WEATHERING THE STORM

KAIT GAMBLE

Weathering the Storm
ISBN # 978-1-78651-875-0
©Copyright Kait Gamble 2016
Cover Art by Posh Gosh ©Copyright March 2016
Interior text design by Claire Siemaszkiewicz
Totally Bound Publishing

Published in 2016 by Totally Bound Publishing, Newland House, The Point, Weaver Road, Lincoln, LN6 3QN, United Kingdom.

Totally Bound Publishing books by Kait Gamble:

Cuffed
Weathering the Storm

The Long Way Round
Grind
Ignite
Scorch

Totally Five Star
Breaking Rossi's Rules
Fuel to the Fire

WEATHERING THE STORM

Dedication

For Roselle

Chapter One

When Maia Reynolds had arrived in Nice, she'd had a list of things she was going to do. Work? Yes. Do some sightseeing and shopping? Absolutely. But coming face to face with the man who abandoned her nearly a decade before and flinging a drink in his face? Definitely not on the itinerary.

She stared at Alexandre Giroux's stunned, dripping face with great satisfaction, and strode out of the restaurant.

No, it hadn't been on the agenda, but it had felt damn good.

She burst out of the building like a cork from a champagne bottle. Sadly, the fizzy, good feeling wasn't to last.

The heavy door slammed and rapid-fire French shouted at her ended the euphoria in a heartbeat.

Maia's determined steps remained unaltered as she hurled over her shoulder, "I don't speak French, remember?"

"How the hell would I know that?" he growled. His long legs closed the distance between them easily as he reached out to snare her.

His hand closed around her arm and he spun her around so she was barely a breath away from his hard form.

Alexandre. So close she could feel the heat of him. Smell him. Sense the ire flaring from him in searing waves as he glared at her with blue-gray eyes as dark as the sea midstorm.

And still, clenched with rage, he was the most handsome man she'd ever seen.

Maia had forgotten how tall and physically dominating he was. How just being in his presence could knock the breath from her lungs. Even as angry as she was, the skin under his hand hummed with awareness. She couldn't stop herself from gravitating toward him — her body still inexorably drawn to his.

Maia balked at the way her body responded to him. After all these years, after what he'd done, he still overwhelmed her senses.

His grip tightened on her arm as he glowered at her from under jet-black eyebrows. "Who are you?"

She glared at him. "Like you don't know. Let me go." Maia tried to shrug out of his grasp but couldn't get loose of his iron-like grip.

Alex turned her toward him again. "Not until you tell me who you are and why you think I need to be publicly humiliated."

Maia stared up into those incredible, penetrating eyes of his and fought away the memories, letting only the anger and hatred through. "Are you kidding me?" She tore her arm out of his grasp and continued her march.

He caught and gripped her hand, anchoring her to the spot. "No, I'm not." His voice was quiet, deadly. It was enough to turn Maia around. They stared at each other for a long moment. "I have no idea who you are."

"Alex?" Neither one of them had noticed that a beautiful dark-haired woman had followed them onto the sidewalk.

"*Ça va*, Angelique." Alex waved her back into the restaurant. She reluctantly obeyed after a long, speculating look at Maia.

Maia shook her head. "You should get back to your date. You wouldn't want her to think that you've abandoned *her*."

He stared at her, eyes narrowed in suspicion. "I might not have a clue who you are, but I suggest you never let me see you again."

"Not a problem." Despite his words, he didn't seem to be in any hurry to let her go. Maia had to claw at his hand to wrench hers from his grip.

Throwing his hand back at him, she stalked away, leaving what she imagined to be a very angry-looking man staring narrow-eyed at her departing form.

It wasn't until she was nearly back at her hotel that she realized that she had left people, *important* people, at the restaurant. She cursed herself. They were probably wondering what had caused her to lash out. Hell, *she* was wondering what had just happened.

Trembling, she raked her shaking hand through her hair. Maia had never let her emotions get the better of her like that before. She prided herself on having perfect control over herself.

Less than five minutes in the same room as Alex and that was shot to hell.

As if she needed further proof the man was toxic.

Maia took a deep breath as she approached the glamorous hotel that was to be her home this week and sighed.

It was over now.

Dumbfounded and furious, Alex watched as the enraged brunette stomped away while his pulse thundered in his ears. What the hell had just happened?

He had walked into the restaurant to enjoy a quiet dinner with his father. There was a writer visiting whom he wanted Alex to meet. He'd mentioned something about them writing an article on the reopening of their hotel. It had been important to his father, so he'd dropped everything and flown in.

One moment he'd spotted his father and was making his way to the table and the next, he'd been soaked by a tiny, spitting mad, brunette wildcat who seemed to think he knew why he'd deserved it.

She was stunning in her fury, whoever she was. The wrathful fire that flared in her dark eyes as she'd scowled at him wasn't something he was used to seeing from women in his company. Nor were the pure hatred and bile. What was she playing at?

Whatever she was thinking, he wasn't about to let her get away with humiliating him the way she had.

Alex's eyes zeroed in on her as she wove determinedly through the crowd. Was she drunk? Insane? He swiped what was left of the champagne off his face and shirt then followed her. He didn't care what her motive was. No one did what she had and walked away from him.

Alex single-mindedly tracked his prey, watching her wind her lithe body easily through the crowd with the dexterity of a dancer. She twisted this way and that, giving him a good idea of the body hidden under the simple black dress. Pert breasts, long, lean legs that led up to a deliciously curved bottom — what the hell was he thinking? His internal rebuke didn't deter the throb of awareness his body had in reaction to watching hers.

There was something about her. The way she felt against him, the way her body fit into his, made him all but forget about Angelique. Everything other than the mystery woman had faded away. He hadn't cared about anything else. But why? He didn't know her. Despite her words, he had no inkling who she was. Yet he wanted to find out more about her. It wasn't an impulse he had very often. Why now? Why her? She'd all but attacked him. The last thing he should feel for her was lust.

Alex shook his head. It wasn't lust he was feeling. It was anger. He wanted retribution.

He stayed a good distance behind her until she reached a familiar sight.

With a sardonic grin on his face, he pulled out his phone as she walked through the entrance.

Oh, how he loved karma.

* * * *

Maia slapped her hand on the flawlessly polished counter, drawing the attention of everyone within earshot of the echoing impact. "What do you mean I can't have my key?"

The wide-eyed man paled and waved helplessly at the phone he'd just put down. "I'm sorry, mademoiselle. I just received a call —"

"From who?"

"From me." The calm voice behind her sent chills skittering up her spine.

Maia turned to face Alex with a sneer. "What do you think you're doing?"

"Getting some answers." He hooked his hand around her elbow and dragged her along as he fired commands at the avidly watching staff.

At the way their eyes dropped and how they immediately went about their business, Maia's stomach started to sink. Alex was someone here with a capital S. "What's going on?"

From the way his jaw was clenched, she wasn't about to get any answers any time soon.

He shoved her headlong into an office and slammed the door closed behind him.

Alexandre's handsome face was twisted with anger. "What is wrong with you? You dare throw your drink at me without provocation? What makes you think you could do that without consequence? I want you out of this hotel!"

Where did he get off barking orders at her? Maia bristled at his tone, but kept herself from yelling right back at him. "Fine by me. Just give me my key and I will."

He stood firm, studying her. "Is this something you usually do? Attack strangers, claiming they did something horrible to you? Goodness knows I've dealt with my fair share of gold-diggers and the like. But you're something else. Is this some sort of angle? A new trick?"

Maia's jaw dropped. He thought it was some sort of scheme to get at his money? "Are you insane?"

"Funny. I was going to ask you the same thing."

"*Monsieur* Girard?" Several staff members appeared with her bags.

Girard? Even as she heard it, Maia scanned the room. First the staff then the walls, which were lined with art as well as photos. Alex featured in several of them. One in particular caught her eye. Alex stood with an older version of himself at a construction site. He was the son of the man she was having dinner with. The owner of this hotel and a half dozen others. That made him Alexandre *Girard*, not *Giroux* as he had told her years ago.

Disgusted with the revelation that he'd lied about his identity, she ignored him. "Are you going to stand there making up crazy things to blame me for all night or are you going to move so I can get out of this place?"

Alexandre slid aside, waving her past. "Good riddance."

"Funny, I was thinking the same thing." Maia smirked as she mimicked his phrasing.

Maia turned and faced him full on. For a long moment, she stared at him. Waited for him to recognize her. Acknowledge their past. Anything. But there was nothing. Not even a flicker.

And it opened up the hole in her chest Maia thought had healed up long ago.

Had she been so easy to forget when it had taken her years to get him out of her head?

Heart aching, she stepped up to Alexandre and stared at him straight in the eyes, searching for any glimmer hinting that all this was just an act. She couldn't find anything other than anger and X-ray-like scrutiny as he tried to figure *her* out.

Maia's heart sank. "You really have no idea who I am, do you?"

His scornful gaze raked over her. "I'm sure I would remember someone as maddening as you."

Maia paid no attention to his tone. "Did you study abroad about eight years ago?"

He glowered. "Yes."

That was something at least. But she wanted him to acknowledge the rest. He knew who she was, he had to. How could he not? So she pressed him. "Don't you remember anything about it?"

His face softened infinitesimally, but Maia caught it before he masked it with a stone-like façade. "No."

"What do you mean, no?" she snarled.

He straightened to his full height and looked imperiously down his nose at her. "About the same time, I was involved in a car accident and lost a portion of my memories. The time I was abroad has a large chunk of the memories gone." He studied her face intently. "I'm told because I haven't been able to recover them that it's probably permanent."

Could she believe him? She searched his eyes again. He stared straight back at her. There was no guile that she could see. Nothing hidden. Could anyone fake something like that?

All her anger exited her body with a heavy breath. The space left behind quickly filled with remorse.

Totally deflated, Maia took a step back. She had just publicly humiliated a man for something he had no recollection of doing. He couldn't remember her or their time together…or anything else. "I apologize for everything. Forget everything I've said and done. I'll leave and that will be that." Maia quickly turned so that he couldn't see the tears threatening to fall. She needed to get away from him.

His large hand closed around her shoulder as he turned her around, gently this time. "Who are you?" Her defiant glare and her silence caused his temper to flare once again. "It doesn't matter. I want you out. I suggest you leave now."

"Miss Reynolds isn't going anywhere, Alex."

"Father—"

Guillaume Girard stepped in between them, gently taking Maia's wrist. He caught what must have been a stricken expression on her face and smiled. "Relax, my dear. I won't bite."

"I'm so sorry—"

His father waved her words away. "No apologies needed, my dear." He turned to address his son. "Miss Reynolds cannot leave the hotel because she is to write an in-depth article about its reopening." He smiled at Maia.

Maia stared at him. Guillaume looked to have the exact opposite reaction to Alexandre. Apparently, a drink thrown at his son amused the older man.

"You can't be serious, Father."

"I am. It was arranged long before tonight. Needless to say, as head architect of the project, you will have to stay on as well, Alex."

Alexandre's jaw clenched but he didn't say a word.

"I'm sure you will want to get some rest after all the excitement. Your editor said she would call you in the morning to settle the details." He clapped his son on the back. "We will meet you for breakfast. Is nine a.m. good for you?"

Maia nodded mechanically.

The older man's smile never waned. "See you then. Goodnight."

Maia raked a hand through her hair. She felt as though she had just been caught in the eye of a hurricane. Somehow, she had managed to make a date with a man she hated.

Chapter Two

Maia couldn't sleep. How could she? The revelation that Alex couldn't remember her chased hundreds of other thoughts whirling through her mind. It changed her perspective on just about everything. She just wasn't ready for that quite yet. Especially since she was stuck with Alex. He was sure to ask questions about why she'd done what she had. Yet another thing she wasn't sure how she should handle at the moment.

Instead of wearing a hole in what was sure to be a very expensive carpet, she opted to head to the pool to burn off some energy. She needed some time to sort out her thoughts and feelings.

Luckily for her, the few other people who had decided to take a late-night dip stayed in the indoor pool.

The one outside sparkled like a sapphire lit from within. The surface winked, beckoning her to dive into its depths. She marveled at how cleverly the infinity edge blended the pool with the ocean in the distance. Wishing she could swim into it and away from her situation, Maia closed her eyes as she took a long, deep breath. The crisp cool air was a far cry from the sultry heat of the afternoon. Perfect for clearing her mind. Maia dropped her robe and dove straight into the deep end.

She loved the water. The moment the cool liquid enveloped her body, Maia's nerves calmed somewhat. Her mind grew tranquil, her thoughts crystalizing. In the water, she could focus on her heartbeat. If only she could spend all her time there.

Maia kicked lazily back to the surface when her lungs started to burn.

As situations went, this had to be the most bizarre she'd ever been stuck in. She was in one of her favorite cities, in a magnificent world-class hotel, and she'd ruined any hopes of enjoying it thanks to what she'd done to Alex. She couldn't even skulk quietly out of town because of the assignment Guillaume and her editor had sorted out. It wasn't exactly something she could turn down. An article like this was a big deal. To say no would be a career killer, especially since Jo would more than likely bust her down to writing horoscopes. Her only alternative was to do her job, keep her head down and try to make it through in one piece.

Even if the thought of being around Alex was slowly making her shrivel up from the inside.

Seeing him again had been a huge shock. Being face to face with him had brought back the festering mess of feelings that she'd thought she'd buried a long time ago, and she'd reacted very badly.

He was handsome — he always had been — but he was even more so now. Grown up, Alex made an impact on her senses in a way that his younger self had been just developing. Alexandre Girard's presence was enough to hush a room and draw gazes. He had the gift of command and he knew how to wield it very well.

His temper hadn't changed. It took a lot to make him lose his composure and getting doused with champagne by a complete stranger was something that would have pushed just about anyone over the edge. She knew he never forgot a slight, and Maia was pretty sure that she'd managed to put herself on his list with one boneheaded move.

Since the article was supposed to be about the hotel and the Girard Group, Maia fervently hoped that she'd be dealing with the senior Girard more than the younger. Thankfully, because of the champagne flinging, she was pretty sure Alexandre wouldn't want to spend more time with her than was absolutely necessary. Who would want to be around someone who had done what she had to him?

That was one blessing at least.

Maia flipped over and cut her way through the water. Just doing something physical felt great. It was incredible how seeing one man again had the ability to tense every muscle in her body. The workout helped to relax them a little.

At the other end, she flipped over again, choosing to float on her back to the other side.

"You shouldn't be down here."

Shivers skittered down her spine at the deep timbre of his voice. But she refused to let herself believe he had been the cause. She'd just been exposed to the cool night air for too long.

Maia opened her eyes to look up at the unimpressed face of Alexandre. She righted herself and held on to the edge of the pool. "Why? Is this your personal swim time?"

He let her snide comment slide. "Actually, I was more concerned about you being out here without a lifeguard."

She hated her knee-jerk reaction. It was obviously going to take some time to learn to let things go. Maia gazed at him, refusing to say another word. They stared at each other for a long moment.

"Miss Reynolds, I want a straight answer to this." He crouched so he could get a good look at her eyes. "Who are you?"

Her attention was caught by the way his trousers pulled taut over his muscular thighs and Maia's mouth went dry. Lifting her gaze to his eyes only made things worse.

She swallowed. "I'm a writer for *Pulse* magazine."

Alex drew a slow breath. "Perhaps you didn't understand me. I don't want to know what you do or where you are from. I want to know how you know about my time abroad and what you think happened during it that made you want to waste perfectly good champagne on my shirt."

Her grip on the ledge tightened. "I'm sorry about that. I apologize. Wholeheartedly."

He didn't move, though he nodded in consideration of her words. "Considering you managed to humiliate me in front of family, friends and press for no good reason, I really don't think you can apologize enough."

Eyes narrowed, she glared at him. "If you want me to grovel, you're going to be waiting a very long time."

He had the gall to look slightly amused at the suggestion. "I don't expect you to kiss my feet. I just want an explanation."

Needing space, Maia pushed off from the side to float away from him. Now was as good a time as any. She took a deep breath. "We dated for a year when we were at university together."

His eyebrows drew together as he processed the information. "And I was such a bad lover that you felt the need to attack me for it nearly a decade later? Try again, Miss Reynolds."

She understood his skepticism, but it still hurt. The memories she had of their time together were some of the best and the worst she had. Biting her lip, she forced a calming breath. "You don't have to believe me, but it's the truth."

His expression hadn't changed. "Let's say what you're saying it true. Why are you so angry with me?"

She closed her eyes against the pain the flood of memories brought back. "You left in the middle of a semester. You said something about something going on with your family. It was all so quick there wasn't time to process what was happening. One minute you were there and the next you were gone. And that was it. You disappeared off the face of the planet."

He contemplated what she had said a moment then shook his head with a wry smile. "Who told you about my amnesia?"

"What?"

"Someone must have told you. How else would you come up with this scheme?" He stared down his nose at her, waiting for a reply.

For a moment, Maia nearly forgot she was in a pool and shock seized her limbs. She quickly recovered before water closed over her nose. Kicking furiously, she glared at him, barely able to put the words together.

"You seriously think I'm making all of this up? What would I have to gain?"

"Money of course. Why else would you come up with something so preposterous? Why is there no evidence of our relationship? If it was as serious as you made it sound, why are there no photos? No mementos?"

Anger hazed her vision as she swam to the opposite side of the pool. She obviously hadn't mattered to him as he had to her, or wouldn't he have kept something? Brought something back with him?

Heart aching, she looked at Alex. "You wanted to know. Now you do. You don't have to believe me. But the next time you want to accuse me of something so disgusting, you can expect something else thrown in your face." Probably her fist.

She levered herself out of the pool and left a sullen Alex watching her leave for the second time.

* * * *

Maia got back to the suite, shivering with cold and suppressed anger. She'd completely forgotten about her robe in her rage and now that it was burning out, the cold had started to seep into her system.

How dare he insinuate she was making everything up to get his money! The idea was repugnant. She had to wonder if he was the one with the diseased mind for coming up with it.

What kind of people did he have to deal with to jump to that sort of conclusion? She shuddered to think.

And he thought she was like them? It infuriated Maia that he thought so little of her.

Maia stalked around the living area like a caged tigress. Her anger and frustration mounted by the second. She couldn't blame him for being cagey when he couldn't remember what had happened, but to throw unmitigated accusations in her face angered her more than anything else he could have done.

Most of all, it made her chest ache in a way she thought she'd gotten over.

Alex didn't remember her. Not that it mattered since this Alex was a far cry from the sweet Alex Giroux she remembered. Then again, the guy she remembered didn't even exist. From all she'd just learned, everything he'd told her as a student had been a lie. Alex was cold, calculating and thought she was a gold-digger. And to top it all off, she was stuck working with him.

Wonderful. Just wonderful.

And, of course, her phone chose that moment to ring.

Jo flashed on the screen as a warning she was about to have a conversation with her boss.

"Hi, Jo." She scrubbed her hand over her face.

Her editor's bubbly voice blasted through the phone. "Maia! I wasn't sure I was going to get you. What time is it over there?"

She couldn't be bothered to check. "I don't know. The sun's not up yet, though."

Jo's tone softened a little, but not by much. "Sorry. Didn't wake you, did I?"

"No." Maia ran a hand through her hair. She got the feeling this was going to be a long one. "I've been told that you wanted to go over the details of the article?"

"Monsieur Girard told you, huh? I thought it would be a great idea to expand on the article." Before Maia could form a retort, her editor barreled on. "I was thinking we could do a themed issue. All the fashion, glamor, nightlife, et cetera, of the French Riviera. I've sent Chloe to you so she can start on the research for the fashion and nightlife. She should be there any time now."

As always, Jo Cannon, Editor in Chief of *Pulse* magazine, was working at breakneck speed. She was what made the magazine such a triumph and her employees such a mess. This wasn't the first time Jo had sprung huge ideas on her. At least this time she had a few hours' heads up.

The only thing she could do was go with it and try not to get knocked over in the process.

Maia took notes while Jo fired a stream of ideas at her and made the appropriate noises at the right times. Or so she hoped. She'd barely heard a word the woman said.

But Jo didn't seem to notice Maia's distracted state. "So it's set, then. I want the article on my desk by the end of the month."

"Great. I'll talk to you again soon." Maia hung up and placed the phone on the table. A whole month in Nice. In other circumstances, she would have been rejoicing. Now, however, the thought of being here a month, working, stuck with Alexandre, only created a sinking feeling in her stomach.

And she had to work with Chloe, the most conniving, backstabbing bitch of a writer she had ever had the misfortune of working with. Maia knew it was only a matter of time before things imploded.

A heavy knock on the door interrupted her silent misery.

Speaking of the witch. Maia yanked open the door to see not only Chloe, but Alex as well.

Maia swept aside and motioned them in. "Chloe. Monsieur Girard."

He waited for the Amazonian blonde to walk in before following. "Miss Reynolds." He gave Maia a slow nod. "Sorry to disturb you. I brought your robe."

Maia took it from him under Chloe's speculating gaze. "Thanks."

Alexandre nodded. "And your colleague wanted to see you right away."

And he'd taken it upon himself to bring her? Maia wasn't quite sure what to make of that. "Thanks again." It sounded flat even to her own ears.

Silence.

It was Chloe who decided to break the heavy silence. "Monsieur Girard here has offered to show me the sights of Nice. Isn't that nice of him?"

"Very." Maia turned to Alexandre. "I've talked to my editor and finalized things with her. If you're going to be occupied" — she spared a glance at Chloe — "all you have to do is give me your notes and I'll take it from there." She fervently hoped that he would take that option so she wouldn't have to suffer his presence again.

He leveled his unnerving gaze on her. "That would be rude of me. My father wanted you to see and know everything about this hotel. How would it look if I abandoned you?"

His choice of wording was like a stab through the heart. "Oh, I'm sure I can handle it."

"Nevertheless, I'll make myself available to you."

How magnanimous of him. She forced a half smile. "Wonderful. I'll see you at breakfast."

"Of course." Then he was gone.

The door closed with a near silent click and her partner for the duration fell against it. "Holy hell, is that man hot." Chloe fanned herself dramatically as she pushed herself off and wandered around the suite. "You should be nicer to him. It's obvious he doesn't like you very much." She sighed as she ran her hand over the glossy glass of the table. "This is a gorgeous room."

Maia just wished the woman gone. "It is."

"Wow. Not a morning person, are you?" Chloe pulled open the curtains to reveal the sun creeping over the horizon.

Not when it was a morning like this one. Shielding her eyes, she sighed. "Chloe, why don't you go explore your room? Maybe take a nap? You know, get on France time."

"Good idea. I'm supposed to meet up with the delectable Monsieur Girard this afternoon so he can show me around a bit." She waggled her eyebrows.

The suggestiveness of Chloe's comment was blatant enough without the eyebrow gymnastics. Maia knew she didn't have the right, but jealousy flared ugly and hot in her gut. "He's out of your league, Chloe."

"Aw, Maia. Don't worry." Chloe patted her on the cheek. "I won't flirt too hard. It shouldn't be too difficult to get the goods from him. After all, he offered to help me. I understand you had to practically get his dad to force him to help you."

Weary, Maia walked to the door and opened it. "Just don't embarrass yourself. Too much."

"I never get embarrassed." Chloe flashed Maia a smile and sashayed out of the room.

Maia believed it.

With a kick, she closed the door, cutting off the wake of whatever perfume Chloe had bathed herself in. She was a piece of work, but with her around, Alexandre would be more than occupied.

The thought gave her hope. She would do the job, be utterly professional and everything would be fine.

She would be fine.

How many times had she told herself that now?

How long before it was true?

Chapter Three

Maia was showered, dressed and reasonably presentable by the time nine a.m. rolled around, but she was resigned to having breakfast looking like a zombie. Who cared, right? It wasn't like she was out to impress anyone.

When she exited the bathroom, she heard a soft knocking at the door.

The smiling face of the older Girard greeted her. "Miss Reynolds! *Bon matin.*"

Maia fought to bring some life to her face. "Good morning, Monsieur Girard. What brings you by?"

"I've talked to your editor and she said that you have a *fantastique* article forthcoming. I'm overjoyed and wanted to thank you in person for agreeing to do it."

She smiled wanly. "You should probably wait until I've written it before you say that."

"Mademoiselle, I have every confidence in you." Guillaume's smile turned apologetic. "I came with the intention of walking with you to breakfast." He blinked at her. "Would you like a few moments?"

Did she look that bad? Maia shook her head. "I was actually just about to go meet your son."

His ever-present smile morphed again, this time turning soft. "I'm sorry that business has impeded on my joining you both this morning. You have to let me make it up to you. Would you agree to dinner at my home tonight?"

Maia didn't want to voice the question that bloomed first and foremost in her mind. Was Alex going to be there? Stupid question. Of course he would be. He was the man's son.

"It will be *fantastique*. I'm having a few friends over for a private celebration for my birthday. You must come."

"I can't think of a reason not to." She really couldn't. Alex be damned. She wasn't about to let him creep back into her life. "It sounds lovely."

"Wonderful! I'll have Alex bring you."

Wouldn't he just love that? "Thank you. Now if you'll please excuse me, I don't want to be late meeting your son. I'm sure he hates me enough as it is."

"Nonsense. Alex will just have to get over it." He crooked his arm at her. "Permit me to walk you to breakfast?"

Maia slipped her arm through his. "Please."

Their progress was punctuated by silence. She was simply too tired to even attempt small talk and Guillaume seemed content to let her brood. At least for a little while.

"You are quiet this morning, Ms. Reynolds," Guillaume said softly.

In an attempt to change the topic she replied, "Please call me Maia, monsieur."

He beamed at her. "Only if you will call me Guillaume. So what has you down?"

She smiled in thanks, though she wasn't quite brave enough to call him by his first name just yet. "I just had a late night."

"Was there a problem with your room?"

She wasn't about to tell him the true reason for her funk. "Oh, nothing like that. I've just had a lot on my mind lately."

"I hope you're not worrying over Alex. He will have gotten over dinner by now."

"But I haven't," she muttered.

Guillaume jostled her good-naturedly. "Come now. What's youth for if not for a little impulsiveness?"

Maia was disinclined to agree.

She was briefly distracted from her self-flagellation by the sight of the terrace as they walked onto it.

The gleaming, white marbled space glowed with the morning sunlight. She could almost imagine she was back in the 1920s as she looked at the intricate wrought iron patterns decorating the door. It was unobtrusive, drawing the gaze to the waves outside or to the arches above the entrance. A perfect touch of glamor.

Her eyes, however, were immediately drawn to Alexandre reading the paper, basking in the sunshine. If the sleeplessness of the night before wore on him, it didn't show. He looked as calm and cool as ever.

"There's Alex now. I'll leave you two to talk." As if he knew she needed the encouragement, he pushed her lightly in the direction of his son. "I will see you tonight."

Mouth dry, Maia nodded and slowly made her way toward the table as if she were walking toward her execution.

"*Bon matin,* Miss Reynolds." Alex didn't even look up from his paper.

Maia would have bristled, but her entire focus was on the glaring headline and photo of her throwing her drink at Alexandre on the front page. Maia cursed herself. She must have been completely enraged for her not to notice any photographers around.

Point made, he folded the paper and placed it innocuously on the table in front of him. "Please sit. Would you like something to eat? To drink?"

Food was the last thing on her mind. "No. Thank you."

She let him help her into her seat. A warm breeze blew as he moved back. It wafted over her, spiced with the scent of the sea and Alex. The memories it evoked sent her stomach into turmoil. No. No breakfast today. And possibly not again until after she left Nice.

He sat and regarded her as closely as she was watching him.

For Maia, it was excruciatingly silent. She'd hoped she could gauge what was going through his mind, but his face was implacable.

"What are you thinking, Miss Reynolds?"

Again, the 'Miss Reynolds' stung, but she forced herself to smile a little when she looked at him again. "I was wondering the same thing about you."

The corner of his mouth lifted. "I was thinking how easily you moved from me to my father." At her incredulous gasp, he continued, "Is he an easier mark for you?"

Bile rose in her throat. "You're a pig. The only reason I'm still here is because your father asked me to write that article."

"So you think that by getting on his good side, you will worm your way into his life."

Her stomach rolled at his accusation. "You are one seriously twisted man. Was it the bump on your head that turned you into" — she gestured at him in disgust — "this?"

"You're saying that as if you know me."

"Obviously, I don't. The man I thought I knew was kind and sweet and would never have jumped to repulsive conclusions like you have."

As she said it, the sense of loss hollowed her again, leaving the sick, unsettled feeling in her gut. Alexandre Giroux had never really existed. She'd been played from the beginning. And she'd been stupid enough to let herself be fooled.

"I'm only stating what I'm seeing."

"What you're seeing isn't the same as what you interpret." She huffed a breath. "If you have anything to discuss that's work related, I suggest you say it now."

"Or you'll leave?"

"How did you guess?"

"Ahh, sarcasm." He reached across the table to slide a white folder to her. "Here is everything you will need to know about my involvement in the reopening."

"Thank you. Is there anything else?" Maia wasn't waiting for an answer. She was already out of her seat when he replied.

"Please stay. Have breakfast. I promise I'll try not to offend."

"No thanks. I'm not hungry." She smirked humorlessly at him. "Or are you afraid your father will scold you for running me out of breakfast?"

"That too." Alexandre levered himself up from his seat and stood, motioning for her to sit back down.

Maia hesitated, but ultimately stayed on her feet. "I should tell him that I can't deal with this. I can't write an unbiased review with you around."

Alexandre frowned. "That won't do. I won't let you disappoint my father."

"I think you've got that wrong. *You're* the one who's disappointing him. You are the one making it impossible for me to work."

That seemed to get him thinking. Maia was within seconds of leaving when he put up his hand. "I apologize."

She raised her eyebrows with a skeptical quirk. "Really? Because it doesn't sound like it."

"I won't say another word if it will mean that you write this article."

His steady gaze held hers. He was being serious.

She stared right back. "You know I won't write anything that's not true. Just because you stay out of my face won't guarantee I will gush about everything."

"I expect nothing else." He motioned at the table. "Will you please sit back down?"

Maia looked around for an excuse and saw the perfect one when she noticed Chloe making a beeline for their table. "No, thanks. But don't worry. It doesn't look like you'll be eating alone."

"Off so soon, Maia?" Chloe edged between Maia and the table and took her seat.

"Yeah, I have work to do."

"Always so serious. You should learn to have a little fun sometime." She turned to Alex and gave him a megawatt smile. "Isn't that right, Alex? Maia never lets herself cut loose."

He smiled at his new companion even as he addressed Maia. "Don't let us keep you from your work, Miss Reynolds."

She turned on her heel and left without another word.

Alex barely heard a thing as the blonde prattled on about her flight...or the last place she'd been before arriving in Nice...or something.

His mind was on another woman and the things she had said.

There was something about Maia Reynolds that told him that what she said was the truth. It made something deep inside ache, even if he couldn't remember her or anything that she mentioned. All he knew was that the pain in her eyes whenever she talked about the past was real. And that hurt something in his chest.

But was *he* really the cause of it?

"Where should we go today, Alex?"

He lifted a shoulder and let it drop again. Alex had little concern with what Chloe did with the day. His interest was with the enigmatic brunette with the fiery temper. "What do you know about Miss Reynolds?"

Chloe pursed her over-glossed lips. "Maia? Why do you care?"

"I'm curious."

She shrugged as she considered his question. It took her a moment before she pouted and shook her head. "There's not much to tell. She's a workaholic. I've heard she keeps a tiny apartment that she's never there to stay in and that she's left a string of broken hearts because she has commitment issues."

His smile was sardonic. "That's quite a bit to know about a woman you claim not to know very well."

She smiled. "I like to know the people I work with."

He toasted her with his juice. "As do I." He took a long sip. "If you'll excuse me, I forgot I have another appointment this morning. Forgive me. We'll have to do this another time."

Alex wanted to retreat to the beach and actually started walking toward it, but the amount of people there kept him near the hotel. Instead, he made his way back up to his suite. The solitude suited his mood as he stood on the wide balcony and stared out at the undulating sea. There was something about the motion of the water that was soothing, hypnotic. It was what he always did when he had to think long and hard.

A knock at the door caught his attention before it opened a crack and his father's head peeked through. "Alex?"

He nodded in greeting. "Papa."

Guillaume picked up on his son's mood and entered quietly. "I just wanted you to know I invited Miss Reynolds to dinner tonight and I need you to bring her."

Dinner? After what had happened this morning, it would be a miracle if Maia was going to still be in the country.

Alex frowned. "Are you sure she agreed? You didn't force her into it, did you?"

Guillaume's eyebrows snapped together. "What are you talking about? Of course I didn't." He joined Alex at the rail. "What is going on between you two?"

Alex turned back to face the sea. For a long moment, he stood silently, listening to the distant sound of water meeting beach. "She hates me."

The lines on the older man's face softened as he chuckled. "Of course she doesn't. Is that what's bothering you? You think she dislikes you?"

"I don't think, Father, I know. She's told me to my face that she hates me. What bothers me the most is I have no idea why." Or why he cared. Alex sighed as he remembered the horrible things he'd accused her of. If Maia hadn't hated him before, he would judge her if she didn't now.

He turned to his father. "While I was abroad or after I returned, did I mention anything about a girl?"

Guillaume thought it over, shaking his head slightly as he did. "Not as such. You were on your independence streak and didn't communicate much while you were away." Guillaume frowned at the memory, and Alex felt a pang of regret for his youthful impudence. "I knew you were interested in returning as soon as possible but you never mentioned a girl, though I would assume no one would be as eager as you to return to just your studies." The older Girard sighed heavily. "That time was such a blur. With your mother ill..."

Alex took in his father's words with a sad scowl. His mother's illness had consumed them both and had taken over their lives for that brief moment in time. It was entirely possible that any other subject had been pushed aside. "Did I bring anything back with me? Photos? A keepsake of some sort?"

"You know you dropped everything to return because your mother was sick. No one was thinking straight. After your accident, I sent Marcel to collect your things and it was all stored away, though you never had any interest in seeing them again."

Of course his father would have sent his PA. He hadn't been in any state of mind to do it himself after the death of his wife, then the accident that had nearly claimed his only son. Marcel was discreet and wouldn't have looked twice at anything unless instructed to. He would have simply overseen that everything was packed up and shipped back, as quickly and efficiently as possible, ready for whenever Alex decided to retrieve it. Only he never had.

Guillaume walked to his son's side. "Now, what is this all about?"

"Maia insists we were lovers for a year during my time at university. That I abandoned her." Alex raked his hands through his hair. "I thought she made it up at first, but now I don't know."

"*Mon dieu.*" Guillaume barely whispered the words as he stared blankly out to sea.

"But when I told her about the accident, she immediately told me to forget what she said. That it didn't matter. But I can see it in her eyes. It matters. Very much. But she refuses to talk about it and even threatened to quit and leave if I push her."

His father's gaze hadn't left the water. "And you think that dinner tonight will do that."

"I think anything that has to do with us breathing the same air might set her off." He turned to his father, sighing as he did.

Guillaume smiled gently at his son. "What can I do to help?"

Alex shook his head bleakly. "I don't know if you can. I doubt if *I* can do anything to sort this mess out."

"Perhaps you should talk to the doctor? I can check to see if your things are still in storage."

Alex shook his head. "Talking to the doctor won't help. He said that if the memories didn't come back after a year, it was quite unlikely that they ever would. I would appreciate if you would ask about my things and whether he ran into Maia back then."

Nodding, Guillaume patted him on the back. "You should sit her down and talk to her. But gently. *C'est le ton qui fait la musique.* A little wine. Dinner. And use some of that Girard charm I know is hiding in there somewhere."

Alex couldn't help but smile a little. His father was a charmer in every way. Unfortunately, he only took after his father physically. If only he had his talent with words.

"Unless you think she's lying." Guillaume clapped his son on the back. "What does your heart tell you?"

Alex didn't know. Only that it hadn't been the same since she'd thrown champagne in his face. "I need to find out more."

"I'll leave it up to you, then."

If only he had the faith in himself that his father did.

Chapter Four

Maia spent the afternoon trying to put words together to describe the fantastically luxurious hotel. The downside of being alone and inside her head was that her mind kept wandering back to Alex.

After so long with Alex out of her mind, she was overwhelmed with thoughts about him. How he'd changed — physically and otherwise. The ridiculous attraction she still felt for him. That even being in the same room with him was too much for her. And now here she was essentially stuck working with him and living at his hotel.

Just a week or two tops. Maybe even less if she could get her act together and just start writing. She had all the info she needed for the article. Alex had been thorough in the information he provided. Paradoxically, it was too much and not enough at the same time. She hated that she wanted to know more about what he did. See him at work.

Maia scowled at the screen as she reread what she'd written. Seeing her thoughts so disjointed just annoyed her even more. Slamming her laptop shut, she decided she needed a break. Not that she had much choice. If her words were anything to go by, it was the only thing she could do right now.

But where to go?

Part of her strategy was to stay in her sanctuary as much as possible to get the job done and get out of here and to her next job.

The less she saw Alex, the better. At least that's what she thought before she realized that he was going to be in her head the whole time.

Maybe a shopping trip would do her some good. She could see some of the area and relax at the same time. Killing two birds with one stone was more appealing than sitting cooped up in her suite, staring at her laptop.

And now she was rationalizing.

So far, nothing about this trip had gone well, so she half expected to see Alex when she stepped into the lobby. It didn't mean she wasn't hoping against it.

He stood at the desk and was already watching her when she noticed him. Not that it was hard to spot him. He was easily the most attractive man in the room and she wasn't the only one who had her eye on him.

He took no notice of anyone else and even smiled a little as he approached her. "Miss Reynolds. I was hoping to catch you."

Pulse fluttering at her throat, she stared at him. And that was how she felt right now. Captured. "Why is that, monsieur?"

"Please, call me Alex."

His gentle tone aroused her suspicions immediately. "What are you playing at?"

"Nothing. I just want us to get along."

"Why?" After the things he'd accused her of, she was sure he'd want to stay as far away from her as possible. Was this about the article? Her hackles started to rise. "You don't have to be nice to me. I'll write a fair piece on the hotel."

He put up his hand. "That's not what this is. Are you always this suspicious of everyone?"

"Can you blame me? Especially after all the vile things you've been accusing me of?" She hadn't always been this way. It wasn't until after he'd disappeared that she'd come to learn that people weren't what you thought they were. "So then what are you doing? It's clear what you think of me. Why else would you want to be anywhere near me? I told you that you could just leave me with any information you want me to include and I'll take it from there. There's no need for you to be involved." Let alone be near enough to scramble her brains any further.

When he stepped closer, she took an instinctive step back.

He halted immediately, a shadow clouding his eyes. "You're afraid of me?"

"Of course not." At least not the way he was obviously thinking. She just didn't want him touching her. It brought back too many feelings. Maia sighed. "I just need to go."

Alex stayed where he was. "Where are you thinking of going?"

"I just need to get some air. And maybe something suitable to wear tonight." She looked up at him. "If you're going to offer to take me—"

He shook his head. "I was, but it's clear that you want nothing to do with me."

What was clear to Maia was that the gentle tone he had started the conversation with was a farce long gone. "I'll see you at the party, I guess."

He pressed his lips in a firm line for a moment. "Be ready by seven. I'll be waiting here."

Right. He was taking her to what sounded like a night of torture. "Fine." She didn't wait for him to say anything else and swept past.

It took a while for her heart rate to return to normal. It didn't help that she hurried out of there as fast as she could and continued the pace until she couldn't see the hotel anymore. Maia knew that holding the past against him wasn't right. The man couldn't remember her. Or what they had. Or…anything. But seeing him brought all the feelings back that she'd thought she had buried forever. And every time she laid eyes on him, it was like running razors over old wounds.

"That can't be Maia, can it?"

Maia sighed at the familiarly irritating voice. The last thing she needed right now was to deal with Chloe. She turned to see the woman heading right for her with an array of bags hanging from each hand.

"And here I thought you never left your laptop."

"Funny." Maia looked up and down the street. She had no idea where to go to find a dress.

"What are you looking for?" Her line of questioning was cut short when her phone started ringing. Chloe rearranged her bags to fish it out of her purse. She barely spared Maia a glance before answering with a delighted giggle. "Monsieur Girard! What a pleasant surprise!"

Of course, he would call *her*. Maia was about to turn and walk away when she saw the beaming grin on Chloe's face extinguish like candlelight in a storm.

"Yes, I'm with her right now." She flicked Maia a disgusted glance. "Yes, of course I'd be more than happy to help her do some shopping." Her words might have been nice but if the expression on her face was anything to go by, Chloe was furious. "I'll see you later, then." She jabbed the button on her phone and dropped it into her purse as if it was tainted. "Come on. Alex thinks you need help shopping."

Maia's spine straightened. She wasn't a child. "I'll be fine."

"He thinks because I'm getting to know the area that I can help you find what you need. I'm not about to let him down, so come on." She stomped ahead clearly expecting Maia to follow.

Maia was about two seconds from turning and walking in the other direction, but she figured it wouldn't hurt to see what Chloe had discovered on her excursions around the city. She was good at finding hidden gems. Besides, being annoyed with her would get her mind off things she'd rather not be thinking about right now. The main thing being a certain tall, dark and infuriating man who seemed determined to get involved in her life one way or another.

On a sigh, she followed Chloe down the narrow sidewalk.

The blonde spare her a glance over her shoulder and rolled her eyes. "Hurry up, will you? I don't have all day. What are you looking for anyway?"

"A dress. Something simple."

"For what?"

The question was obvious. Why would she need a dress when she never went out? "I just need one, okay?"

"Jeez. Touchy much?" She turned back again but this time there was a feral grin on her face. "You're not trying to impress Alex, are you?" She laughed long and hard like it was the funniest thing she'd ever heard.

"Actually I need it for a work thing."

"Did the elder Monsieur Girard invite you to dinner too?"

Why did she think she would be the only one who had been invited? It was a professional thing. Nothing personal. Still, it took the shine off the evening — what little there was of it. Now she'd have to deal with Alex *and* Chloe. Oh, joy.

She shrugged as nonchalantly as she could. "Yeah. And since I've already used up the only good dress I have with me for dinner with him the other night, I thought I'd buy something new."

"And update that so-called wardrobe of yours at the same time, right?" She snickered.

Maia wasn't going to argue with her. She liked to buy classic pieces that she could mix and match. Quality over quantity and all that. She traveled so much that it was just easier to keep the amount of clothes she took with her to a minimum where everything was her favorite. Unlike Chloe, who jumped on every trend and clung on with her acrylic-tipped nails until there was something newer and, in her eyes, better.

Maybe she could just find something to augment what she'd brought with her. She was always on the lookout for new jewelry or accessories. This trip, however, was about buying whatever she could find first. The less time spent with Chloe the better. Then she could finally have some time to enjoy on her own before being dragged to that dinner.

Even the prospect of having to be in the same room as Alex for a couple of hours sucked the life out of her. It was going to be pure torture.

"Hey, snap out of it. See if you can find anything in here." Chloe pointed at a garish-looking shop.

Who could have thought shopping could be less fun?

Chapter Five

By the time Maia was able to find what she wanted, Chloe had found and bought five times the number of items to add to her stack of purchases. And it wasn't until they were on their way back that Chloe said anything that was remotely interesting.

"He's asked about you."

Maia hadn't been listening to anything she'd been saying up to that point and was perfectly content with counting cars and cracks on the sidewalk. "Who?"

"Alex Girard."

Trust Chloe to bring up the one person she didn't want to think about. "Why?"

"How should I know? He asked what I knew about you."

Thankfully, Chloe didn't know very much about her past. Or her life in general. Maia shrugged. "So I guess you told him you know nothing about me?"

"I told him what I know. That you were anti-relationship and you never have fun."

"Great." Perfect. Maybe that would put him off from trying to get closer.

Chloe shrugged. "It's only the truth. What I don't get is why he even wants to know?" There was a pause just before her lips curved and a gleam appeared in her eyes. "I wonder if he's one of those guys who are into the chase. That would explain why he's curious about you." She looked Maia up and down. "Then again, he could be worried that you'll attack him with something worse than champagne next time."

"He doesn't have to worry about that. I just want to do my job and get out of here."

Chloe grinned. "I guess I don't have to worry about competing with you. Not that I did in the first place."

Maia didn't know why Chloe was so hostile toward her and she didn't care. She wasn't going to get into an argument with her and she sure as hell wasn't going to fight with her over a man. Least of all, Alex.

"Nothing to say?" Chloe shifted her bags. "Why did you throw the champagne at him anyway?"

Thankfully, the hotel was in view and Maia quickened her pace. "I tripped."

"We both know that's a lie." She twisted her lips. "The truth will come out soon enough."

Not before she got out of there and never had to see Alex again. "Whatever. I'll see you at dinner." Maia stalked off. It was going to take solitude and maybe even a bath to get her head ready to deal with the coming evening.

* * * *

It took a large glass of very expensive wine, a warm bath laced with oils provided by the hotel in tall, elegantly carved bottles, and several wardrobe changes before Maia was ready. She probably would have changed the earrings one more time but a knock at her door stopped her.

Alex stood on the other side, dressed impeccably in a dark suit and white shirt. Only this time there was no tie and the shirt's top button was undone. Maia's eyes were drawn to the exposed skin for an extended moment.

"Are you ready?" His gaze traveled the length of her body.

Not in the least. Didn't he say he was going to wait for her at the desk? She had at least ten minutes by her count. But Maia didn't question it. The less said, the better.

"Just let me get my shoes." Maia quickly dug a pair of simple black Manolos out of her suitcase and slipped them on. With one last look in the mirror, she grabbed her purse and nodded to him. "Ready."

Keeping pace with him, Maia stayed stubbornly quiet as they walked down the hall. She wanted to look at him and kept sneaking peeks at him when she was sure he wasn't looking. Not that he would be. What did he care if she did? She'd just be one of many.

Maia thought glumly of the gorgeous woman who had been with him at the restaurant. He was probably dating her, and possibly a string of others now anyway.

By the time they reached the entrance, Maia's spirits were at an all-time low, even for this trip. The last thing she wanted to do was go to a party.

"You're quiet."

It took her a second to realize that Alex was talking to her. And another to notice that he'd stopped while she'd kept going. "I have a lot on my mind. With the assignment and all," she finished lamely. Why did she have to explain herself to him anyway? She owed him nothing.

Something that appeared to be like concern curved his lips downward. "Don't feel obligated to come to the party just because my father asked. If you're not up for it, just say so."

She'd already thought about it, but had decided it would be best to go. "I already told him I was going to attend. I don't want to let him down."

Alex simply shrugged and started walking again.

Maia followed.

They didn't have far to go. On the circular path just outside the foyer doors waited a sleek black car that could have been something out of the future.

Alex quickly opened the passenger side door and held out his hand. Maia took it and slid into the seat, pulling her hand back the moment she was in. He circled around and was about to get in his side when a clatter of heels and a flash of blonde dashed toward him.

"Alex! I'm so glad I caught you. I tried calling for a cab but, unfortunately, they're all tied up right now. So I was wondering…" She nibbled on her bottom lip and batted her lashes.

Chloe really had no shame.

Alex shrugged. "There's no room for you in this car, I'm afraid." He glanced pointedly at his seat then at Maia in the other.

Chloe leaned over and made a show of spotting her coworker. "Oh, hi, Maia. Didn't see you there."

"You know what? You take Chloe. I'm going to get some work done. Maybe swim a few laps." Or crawl into bed and sleep until the nightmare was over.

Alex circled around and dutifully helped her out. "I have a solution that will get us all there. After all, didn't you say you didn't want to disappoint my father?"

Alex might have been an ass, but Guillaume didn't deserve to be let down.

She didn't get to answer. He'd already pulled his phone out and was directing someone on the other end. Maia spared Chloe a glance to see the blonde's triumphant expression.

Congratulations. Chloe had gotten her out of a situation she didn't want to be in in the first place.

Within minutes, a black limo pulled up. The driver quickly opened the door and Chloe was the first in. Maia followed then Alex.

Then started the most awkward limo ride Maia had ever experienced. Most of the time, she enjoyed not having to drive herself and appreciating the view from a limo wasn't the worst way to travel. But now she sat stiffly in her seat, her knees angled toward the door as she did her best to disappear. Chloe, on the other hand, eyed the little refrigerator and Alex with equal interest even though the man took no notice of her.

He'd chosen the seat next to Maia. Though he didn't encroach on her space or engage her in conversation, Maia was still overwhelmed. She could smell the spice of his cologne. Feel the heat emanating from him. Awareness flooded her body like molten honey in response and it twisted her insides into knots.

She did her best to avoid contact, to ignore him. That was until the car turned sharply, sending her toppling into Alex's solid body. Maia's brain blanked the moment his strong arms closed around her.

He held her against his hard form for a second before easing her back to study her. "Are you okay?"

Her brain kick-started back to life and she slid away, as far from him as she could. "I'm fine. Thanks."

"I'm good too, you know." Chloe watched them with blatant interest.

"Good." Alex didn't even glance at her. His eyes stayed on Maia until Chloe started talking again.

She smirked at Alex. "I guess I should stop wasting my time with you, huh?"

He turned his gaze to her, but he said nothing.

"I don't know what's going on between you two but there's definitely something." Chloe narrowed her eyes suspiciously. She looked as though she had been going to say something else but had thought better of it.

And knowing Chloe, she had a lot to say.

Maia sat stiffly against the door until the car eventually slowed and stopped. Alex exited first and helped her and Chloe out of the car respectfully.

She wasn't sure what she had expected to be walking into when she had been invited to a party at Guillaume Girard's home, but she was greeted by a dozen people all chatting and mingling inside and out of the gorgeous villa. Alex led them through while Chloe disappeared into the crowd almost immediately.

Maia saw the moment Guillaume spotted them. He wove through the crowd to them with a big grin on his face. "Alex! Maia! So glad you're here."

He clapped his son on the shoulder and kissed Maia on one cheek then the other. "Come, I have some people for you to meet." He waved at a waiter, who immediately approached with a silver tray heavy with gleaming glasses of champagne.

Maia took one with no intention of drinking any of it. It probably would have tasted like sawdust anyway. She noticed that Alex refused a drink. He followed along quietly as Guillaume made a beeline through the throng.

She couldn't keep names straight as he introduced her to one person after another. Alex seemed to know everyone. Men and women alike were eager to snare him in conversation. She listened while he made what she assumed was polite conversation in half a dozen languages. Maia smiled and chatted, and actually began to enjoy herself. That was until Chloe made her way back over.

"Maia! You'll never guess what just happened to me!"

The huge grin on her face made Maia's stomach roll. And when she saw who Chloe dragged behind her, it fell to her feet.

"I was telling this gorgeous man what I do for a living and that I was here with the stunningly fabulous Maia Reynolds and apparently he knows you!"

Tall, broad, handsome, dirty blond. Tonight he wore a navy suit and a delighted grin at seeing her. Of course she knew Tomas Baer. They'd dated for a few months before he'd decided he wanted to take things further and she had done the only thing she could think of at the time — run.

If he was angry, it certainly didn't show. He took her hand and squeezed. "Maia. How good to see you again."

"Tomas. What are you doing here?" Her heart threatened to pound its way out of her chest as she felt Alex step up next to her.

"Why don't we leave these two to catch up, Alex?" Chloe beamed up at him as she linked her arm through his and pulled him away.

Alex glanced at Maia as if he was making sure she was okay. When she managed a nod, he let Chloe lead him through the crowd.

"Imagine my surprise when Chloe told me she worked with you." Tomas' vivid blue gaze roamed down over her and back until his eyes met hers again. "You've been keeping well."

"You look…" *Great. Fantastic.* "Good too." After Alex, Tomas was the closest anyone had ever gotten to her heart. She gently pulled her hand from his grip. "So what are you doing here?"

"I'm an investor with the Girard Group. Chloe mentioned you were working on an article about the refurbishment of their most luxurious hotel. What a coincidence."

Quite. "It's strange how things work out, isn't it?"

He smiled just as Guillaume waved everyone into the dining room. "It seems that dinner is served."

Everyone convened at the huge, elegantly set table. Maia couldn't help but notice the beautiful place settings. Whomever Guillaume had hired to set up the tables had done a spectacular job.

The theme, it seemed, was the ocean. The greens and blues of the plates mixed well with the cream-colored tablecloth. Along the center of the table were several centerpieces constructed of seashells of every size, variety and color set around whorled candle holders that looked like waves lit from within.

Maia would have been enchanted if she hadn't been so stressed out.

Alex and Guillaume took the ends. Maia sat next to Alex and Tomas claimed the seat on the other side of her before anyone else could. Chloe sat directly across from them looking as though she'd claimed a front row seat to a championship match.

So much for her somewhat enjoyable evening.

The food was wonderful, or so everyone kept saying. She was sure it was. The meal looked incredible. To keep with the theme, every variety of seafood she could imagine was appealingly presented. Lobster, jumbo shrimp, fish, clams and oysters were served up in a mindboggling number of ways.

Too bad Maia just didn't have much of an appetite and what she did manage to get down tasted like straw. To add to her distress, Tomas, for whatever reason, decided to act like the doting boyfriend and placed morsels of food onto her plate that she 'just had to try'.

Not wanting to cause a scene, Maia just let him. He never even noticed that she didn't touch a thing he'd given her.

Alex, on her other side, barely said a word, but she sensed the tension in him. She wondered what he might be thinking. After all the things he'd accused her of, this probably was the proof he needed to peg her as a lying gold-digger.

What did she care if he did? He could think whatever he wanted.

She speared something green on her plate and stuck it in her mouth, chewing it as if it was another one of Alex's crazy accusations.

Then Maia nearly choked on it when he gently put his hand on hers. "Maia?"

His touch snapped her attention back to the present. Everyone looked at her, clearly waiting for an answer to a question she hadn't heard. Her eyes immediately went to Alex. What had she missed?

Guillaume's gaze was on their joined hands before it slid up to meet hers. "I asked how you were coming along with the article, my dear."

"Oh." She tried to pull her hand away from Alex's, but his grip tightened. Maia gave up and let it lay limp beneath his. "I've been sifting through the information that Alexandre gave me. The rebuild of the hotel and the glamor of it then and now is remarkable. It definitely won't be hard to write the article. I think it'll be a great one once I'm done."

"Maia always writes great pieces," volunteered Chloe. "Her whole life revolves around work so it's not like she has anything to distract her."

Maia could feel all eyes turn to her again. The ones from either side of her burned the most. What surprised her was Tomas had a response to that.

"If you knew Maia at all, you would know that there is more to her than work. People are icebergs. You only ever get to see a tiny bit on the surface when the true person is the larger part hidden below. Especially if you don't take time to get to know them." He then continued to eat as if the exchange hadn't even happened.

After what she'd done to him, Tomas was the last person she would expect to come to her defense.

Maia kept the wan smile on her face as she made another attempt to eat. Thankfully, Alex had taken his hand from hers. She snuck a glance at him to find that he was already watching her with speculating interest and a mysterious half smile.

The rest of the meal went by without Chloe saying anything else snide about Maia. Instead, she did her best to turn the conversation to her favorite topic—herself. Maia was relieved. With everyone focused on

Chloe, she'd be too occupied to make any more comments.

As the meal came to an end, people drifted off into separate little groups. Maia took advantage of Tomas and Alex being distracted by other guests who vied for their attentions. Fully intending to use the moment to catch her breath, Maia edged toward the veranda.

"I hope you're enjoying yourself, Maia." Guillaume approached her with a friendly smile.

Caught, she forced a cheery grin. "I am. Thank you for inviting me." What else could she say?

Guillaume motioned to the bar laden with dozens of bottles. "Can I make you anything?" When she shook her head, he smiled and walked them to the veranda as if he knew that she needed space more than anything else right now.

Maia inhaled the cool night air, enjoying the blended scents of sea and exotic wild flowers. Another two breaths and she felt almost normal.

"So Alex tells me that you two have a past."

Maia nearly choked on her next breath. He'd spoken to his father about her? It wasn't too hard to believe considering the champagne incident. It would only be natural to wonder why it had happened.

It took her a long moment to formulate her reply. "That's just what it was. The past."

"I see." He brooded quietly for a moment. Maia blinked. It was like she was getting a glimpse of Alex in the future. "Can I tell you something, Maia?"

Maia's heart fluttered. Did she really want to hear what he had to say? She nodded stiffly.

"Alex and I didn't have the greatest relationship when he was growing up. I'm sure you can see he's quite bull-headed and single-minded in his determination." He chuckled when Maia only stared back wide-eyed, unwilling to respond to that. "He was much worse when he was younger. He resented having doors opened for him. He was very determined to make it on his own, hence his move abroad for his schooling."

Maia remembered he never really mentioned his parents when they were together. Whenever they came up, he'd tense up and change the subject.

"Alex refused to come home for the holidays. He didn't even want to talk to us on the phone. I don't think he planned on coming back until he'd made his first million. But then his mother grew ill." Guillaume's smile waned a little and he cleared his throat. "After the accident, Alex became a different person. It was almost as if he lost a part of himself along with the memories. He became hard. Distant. His studies, then afterward work became his life." He looked at her as if he recognized something in her eyes.

Maia knew what it was he saw. She was the same. After Alex left, she'd closed herself off, focused on her studies and, after graduation, did nothing but work. "Why are you telling me this?"

His voice was soft. "I think that you two can help each other."

"I don't think that we can." Maia gripped the stone railing with both hands. "I don't think I can."

"I don't mean to push." Guillaume put a gentle hand on her shoulder. "Or pry. I just see the way you two look at each other." His smile widened when she whipped her head around to gape at him. "There is still something there."

Alex saw his father and Maia talking on the veranda and wondered what they could be discussing. From a glance at Maia, he'd have to say it wasn't about the article. When a pained expression briefly darkened her exquisite features, he had a sneaking suspicion that they were talking about him.

He took a step toward them with a sudden, but inexplicable need to coax the look off her face.

"Alex."

Tomas approached with a glass of brandy in each hand.

"Tomas. Good to see you again." He took the offered drink. For a long while, the two men stood silently taking stock of each other.

"So you and Maia, huh?" Tomas waded into the conversation slowly, between sips of the golden liquid. "Sorry if I stepped on your toes at dinner. I didn't know you and she were a thing."

Alex wasn't sure why he didn't correct his friend. He didn't dwell on it. Instead, he focused on what he saw between Tomas and Maia. "You two were together once."

The blond man nodded. "About a year ago." He smiled sadly. "I have to admit when I first saw her this evening, I thought this was my second chance. I guess I thought wrong."

Alex shrugged nonchalantly, but he studied the other man, his words, his actions as he spoke of Maia. He clearly still had feelings. "Why did you two break up?"

"She left me. It was my fault. I knew Maia had a problem with commitment." He sighed. "To put it in the most basic terms, I pushed and she ran."

He said it so simply. So plainly. As if he were stating that her hair was brown, or that her eyes were hazel. It seemed that Chloe's assessment of her coworker was accurate enough.

"You don't seem to hold a grudge." Alex wasn't sure he could be so magnanimous if their roles were reversed.

"Like I said, it was my fault." He looked Alex up and down again. "I've been waiting for her, but I guess it's pointless now that you two are together."

Again, Alex let his friend's assumption pass. "Did you ever find out why she was so reluctant to settle down with you?"

Tomas downed the last of his drink and shook his head. "Not exactly. I'm sure you've noticed that Maia doesn't like to talk about feelings. It wasn't until just before she left that she confided that she'd been hurt in the past and was afraid and unwilling to open herself up that way again." He shrugged. "I was the idiot who drove her away. Only I had hoped she would find her way back to me. You're a lucky man, Alex." Tomas clapped his friend on the shoulder.

Alex felt a pang for his friend. "Things don't always work out the way we want. I'm sorry, my friend." *Not really.*

"I'll be fine. Just glad she didn't end up with a creep who will take advantage of her." He chuckled humorlessly. "Or someone like the *arschloch* that messed her up so badly."

Something that felt faintly like guilt twisted at his gut. Was he the one to turn her into the commitment-phobic woman she now was? If so, it was up to him to make things right. "Did she mention what he did to her?"

Tomas shook his head. "That was one thing she would never talk about. Whatever it was it made her stop trusting men with her heart." He smiled. "Perhaps you will be the one to shatter that shell."

Not likely if he was the one who had put it there.

Tomas took a healthy sip of the amber liquid as he regarded Alex. "So how are the projects in Asia coming along?"

Alex smiled. At last. Something he knew and could discuss with some intelligence.

Chapter Six

Maia opted to stay outside a little longer to enjoy the cool air, the view and the solitude—to mull over the new information.

Guillaume left her with a few thoughts. None of them were about helping Alex heal. Most of them included escape or hiding until her job was done. And staying away from him. The farther she kept from Alex, the better for her sanity. What frightened her most was the attraction she still felt for him. It wasn't logical. He'd hurt her so badly and yet her hormones still ran amuck whenever she got near him.

"Maia." Tomas approached her cautiously, as if he was afraid she was going to turn and run like a frightened rabbit.

Not that she could blame him.

"Hi." She looked back out over the ocean before turning back to him again. Tomas was gorgeous. Sweet. Caring. Kind. Definitely a man for whom she could imagine letting her guard down. And if she had stayed with him, she probably could have, eventually. But after seeing Alex again, Tomas' presence, no matter how dazzling, was eclipsed. She put a hand on his and took a deep breath. "I'm sorry about what I did to you. To us."

He enclosed her hand between his. "I know, Maia. I can't say I wasn't angry. And disappointed. I thought what we had was worth working for. Fighting for. When you took off the way you did, I went a little crazy. I tried to find you. And when I couldn't..." He took her hand and pressed it to his chest. "I realized that if you wanted me, you would come back."

And that was the moment she realized that what she had done to Tomas was what she thought Alex had done to her. It made her heart shrivel to think that she had done it deliberately. She might not have been thinking straight and had been only following her instincts, but she had still abandoned a man who so had obviously cared for her. Alex had had an excuse. What did she have? A messed-up head? It brought anguished tears to her eyes that she had hurt him the way she had.

"You don't have to say anything. I can see that you and Alex are together. I want you to be happy and if it's with him then I'm okay with that."

Maia's heart clenched. He had things so wrong in that regard, but she didn't correct him. "Tomas... I'm so sorry." That at least was the truth. "I was a coward. And I never should have run out on you like that. I hate that I hurt you. I should have called or texted or...something."

He wiped away her tears with his thumb. "Hey, now. Whatever will be, will be."

It was his philosophy and was one of the reasons she got along so well with him. It was also what frightened her. Things with him were comfortable. Easy. He just wasn't what she wanted. Who she wanted. She didn't think she could want anyone ever again. At least, not the forever kind.

"Now that I know you are well, I'm fine." His smile was a little sad as he let his hand drop. "Think of me from time to time, *liebling*."

Maia nodded. How could she forget about someone so sweet?

He left her then, and for a long time, all she heard were the muted sounds of conversation in the background while the breeze whispered around her.

She had known for years that she was damaged. After Alex had disappeared, she'd found it hard to trust anyone. There'd only been a few attempts at a relationship over the years and they'd all failed because she wouldn't let her walls down. The last was with Tomas. It hadn't been easy to walk away from him. He'd been the closest she'd come to truly opening up to anyone in a very long time.

Only she hadn't been able to. And she'd hurt a good man.

Disgusted with herself, she gripped the balustrade and stared into the distance. The realization of her own sickening actions had to come after she found out that everything she believed about Alex's abandonment of her was wrong. That he wasn't to blame.

He didn't remember her. Or anything they had. Or shared. And she was left with nothing but bitter memories.

It was a cruel trick of fate.

It was sad. And it left her a seething mess of confused emotions.

The tears built and she gritted her teeth against them. She wasn't going to cry. She wasn't going to break down.

She felt his presence before she heard him.

"Maia? Are you okay?"

Not really. She nodded. "I'm fine."

Alex spun her around and gently cupped her cheek. "You don't look fine."

His touch triggered her impulse to run. Blood roared in her ears. She tried to back away but was trapped against the railing. "Alex. Please. Just leave me alone."

"I can't." He tipped her chin up so she had no choice but to look up into his eyes. "You've done your damnedest to push me away, but for some reason I just can't get you out of my head. I'm not going to let you drive me away, especially not when you're upset."

Alex's gaze was hypnotic, heated, as he peered into her eyes. "When you threw that drink at me at the restaurant, I thought you were insane. When you told me that we had been together in the past, I thought you were lying." Alex touched her cheek with his fingertips. "But I haven't been able to stop thinking about you." His touch made her skin tingle, just like it always had. Maia was on the verge of turning her face into his palm, but forced herself to twist out of his grasp. To put some space between them.

"Well, you should. Just forget about me."

He stepped closer, but didn't touch her this time. "I can't. I won't. There's something about you that I can't ignore."

What could she say to that? It was what she'd thought she wanted all those years ago, but now? She was too messed up to even contemplate another relationship, let alone one with Alex.

"Don't say anything. I'm not going to push you. I just want the chance to get to know you."

"Why? I attacked you. I'm obviously unable to maintain a lasting relationship. I'm sure you've heard that by now." It just didn't make sense for him to be interested in her. Especially when he could have any woman he wanted.

"Like I said, there's something about you." He dropped his head to lightly brush her lips with his. "Something I want."

It was a ghost of a kiss, but Maia's body reacted as if her blood had been ignited. He brushed his mouth over hers gently before darting his tongue out to taste her lips. The instant he did, she gasped at the intense sensation from the glancing contact.

Alex took quick advantage and deepened the kiss, angling her back so he could devour her.

Maia clung to his shoulders as their tongues dueled. Instinctively, she pressed against his hard chest, reveling in the strength she found there. His arms held her firmly against him, refusing any space between them.

A long-forgotten sensation took hold. Heat blasted through her body from every point he touched to pool low in her pelvis in a liquid ache. She wanted him with a ferocity that shook her from head to toe.

It was as exhilarating as it was terrifying.

Trembling she shuffled back. Licking her lips, getting that one last taste of him, she fought to get her breathing back under control. "Alex... I don't know if this is such a good idea."

It would be too easy to let him do what he liked. But if she did, then it would leave her wide open to getting hurt once more. And if things went wrong with them yet again, would she be able to put herself back together?

He closed his hands over hers and grazed her lips, her chin then her earlobe with his lips to whisper, "Trust me."

That was the problem. She had before and it had nearly destroyed her.

Chapter Seven

Maia woke the next morning still in a daze. On the way back to the hotel, Alex hadn't said anything more about the subject of them. He had walked her to her door, kissed her hand gently and bidden her goodnight.

She had floated to bed and, in her dreams, she'd been back at university and they'd been basking in the glow of young love.

The dreamy haze fizzled away in the sobering morning light and was replaced by confusion, which was then quickly chased by trepidation.

What was he thinking? Had he talked to Tomas? What had he told Alex? What had Chloe been telling him?

Why did she care?

He might have been interested in starting things up again, but she wasn't.

Maia dialed room service and pulled out her laptop. She was going to write the article and get out of there before she did something monumentally stupid.

Like let herself fall for Alex again.

* * * *

By the time breakfast arrived, Maia had manically put together a third of the article. If she worked through the day, she could have a fantastic first draft done. By midnight, she might even have approval from Jo. Within twenty-four hours, she could be on a plane headed to the other side of the planet.

Bolstered by the idea, Maia had a grin on her face when she opened the door only to have it melt away when she saw who had brought her meal.

"Morning, Maia." Alex smiled and deftly sidestepped her as he walked into the suite.

"What are you doing here?" She ran a hand through her tangle of hair reflexively. Maia hadn't anticipated him showing up like this.

"I thought I would bring you breakfast since I didn't see you downstairs this morning." He uncovered the tray. "I hope this is to your liking. You strike me as a fruit for breakfast kind of person."

He was right about that. It looked wonderful. "Thanks, but I ordered room service."

"Let me worry about that." If he noticed she looked like she'd just fallen out of bed, he didn't say anything. Instead, he ushered her to the seat and sat her down. He then pushed back the curtains and opened the balcony doors with a flourish.

It was only when he sat and picked up a cup of coffee that she noticed there were two. It looked like it was going to be more than him simply dropping off the food then leaving. Then again, had she ever really thought that it was even a possibility?

"Don't be shy." Alex speared a plump strawberry and handed her the fork. "How's the article coming along?"

Of course, he would have seen the laptop. She took the fork and put it back down in favor of the coffee. "Good. I think I can be finished with the first draft tonight."

He took a slow sip of his coffee and took his time swallowing. "That soon?"

She followed his lead and sipped out of her own cup before she answered. "Yes. Jo's been talking of another article about a new game lodge in South Africa. The villas are situated on the reserve grounds up in the trees so animals can come right up to your window. Definitely not for the faint of heart. I can't wait. It's been a while since I've been chased by wild animals." She laughed. "She wants me there ASAP."

Truth was, she had been the one thinking about running the idea past Jo. It seemed like the best place to go to get away from everything and get her head together. The sooner the better.

Alex held her gaze steadily. "What if I told you that I know of another radical hotel that no one else knows about and that it's much better? And that I can give you exclusive access?"

That made her pause mid-chew. Curiosity on the rise, she carefully swallowed the succulent melon. "Really? Where is it? What makes it better than giraffes at your window or lions wandering past your villa?"

"Well, there is less of a chance that you'll be eaten, for one." He smiled and impaled a bit of kiwi. "Are you interested in seeing it?"

He knew he had her, Maia could see it in his smile. How could she say no? She was practically salivating at the idea of seeing something no one else even had an inkling about.

She did her best to appear calm and businesslike, though she had to concentrate to keep herself from bouncing out of her seat. "I need to know a little more before I can answer. I'm assuming it's a project that the Girard Group is working on."

Alex slung his arm over the back of the chair. "Naturally."

He was enjoying teasing her. Baiting her. The slight smirk was the only indication that she needed.

She took a leisurely sip of her coffee. "Will you at least tell me where it is?"

Alex leaned in. "Imagine paradise."

Not one to back down, Maia leaned closer as well. "I have a very vivid imagination. The word 'paradise' can encompass a lot. I want facts, not fantasy."

The smirk on his face grew. "How about I arrange for a visit? If you have time in your busy schedule, that is."

Maia nodded. "I'll have to make a few calls, but I don't see there being a problem."

The smile turned satisfied. "Wonderful. I'll sort out the details and will get back to you. Are you enjoying your breakfast?"

"I am." Maia took another bite to prove it. "Are you going to tell me anything about your new hotel?"

"No."

She smiled around her fork.

"Just think of it as going on an adventure."

It *was* an adventure. Then the idea started to sink in. She didn't know where they were going. Or who else would be there. Would they be alone? She wasn't sure if she could handle that. "Will your father be coming? Maybe Chloe should come along too?"

"Are you afraid of being alone with me, Maia?"

Her eyes met his and for an instant, she was sure he was reading her mind. "No."

"Good, because you shouldn't be. I'll see what my father thinks, of course. But we shouldn't bother Chloe. There isn't much for her there. It's not her kind of resort."

Maia didn't want her there anyway, but she figured any buffer was better than none. "I guess it wouldn't be." She stuffed the remainder of her meal into her mouth. "Thank you for breakfast."

"You're very welcome." He made no move to leave.

Maia pushed the plate closer toward him, hoping he would take the hint.

He didn't.

Alex leisurely sipped the last of his coffee and placed it on the table. "I thought we could spend a little time together. I could show you around the hotel. I know more about the refurbishment than anyone, except perhaps my father."

Of course he would. He was the head architect on the project. Picking his brain about little details did appeal to her. At least the intellectual side of her. Her ambitious side.

Giving him a small, apologetic shrug, she looked down at herself before turning her gaze back to him. "If you give me a few minutes, I'd be glad to join you."

Alex nodded, but still didn't take the hint that she wanted him out of the room. At least for the moment. Instead, he pulled out his phone. "I'll be on the balcony."

At least he was out of her way.

Alex stared out at the ocean. He hadn't meant to give away the new project. Although it was almost ready for opening, there were a few kinks that had to be worked out before he would allow an announcement. But hearing Maia's plans to get away from him so soon had triggered a gut reaction. He had to find a way to make her stay. To find a way for them to spend more time together.

Teasing her with the new resort seemed to be the only thing he could entice her with. But he was willing to do just about anything to keep her around just a little while longer.

After dropping her off the night before, he'd had a hell of a time getting to sleep. He had found himself dwelling on what Tomas had told him about Maia. That, and the woman herself. Maia had looked stunning, if a little pale and apprehensive of the party. He hadn't been able to keep his eyes off her. When the car had swerved around the corner and sent her careening into him, he'd felt a flare of awareness that hadn't subsided the entire night.

Watching Tomas fawn over her hadn't settled well. He'd never thought of himself as a territorial man, but seeing his friend take care of Maia had created a potent ball of fury in his gut that had caught him off guard. He'd never felt the urge to punch another man because of a woman before—he'd never had to—but he'd come close to it last night. Very close.

Alex shook it off and turned, leaning against the railing. He caught a glimpse of Maia in the bathroom as he pulled out his phone but he dropped it back in his pocket as his fingers suddenly malfunctioned. The sight of her in bra and panties, even the sliver of her that he'd seen, was tantalizing and shot blood straight to his groin. It made him wonder what it would be like to have her look at him without the apprehension in her eyes. Or how she would look under him flushed and in the throes of passion.

Turning away again, he gripped the rail, trying to get his head and libido under control. He hadn't been lying when he'd told her that she made him feel something. He just wasn't sure what exactly it was that he felt. What Alex did know was that he wasn't ready to let her go. Not until he figured it out.

He fished out his phone again and dialed.

Maia rushed through her usual morning routine. She showered, dressed and put on a light layer of makeup. By the time she felt ready to face him, she was pulling her still damp hair into a ponytail. When she walked back into the living space, Alex stepped back into the room, wafting in with him the tantalizing scent of the sea and morning sun.

His gaze traveled down her body and he smiled appreciatively as it made the return trip up. "You look wonderful."

Maia wouldn't admit it but she had made a tiny bit more of an effort than she usually would when she was spending the day on her own. Of course she had. She would be all over the hotel. It didn't hurt to make a good impression. Because that's why she'd done it.

She toyed with the earrings she'd had to dig through her suitcase to find. "Thanks." She paused when she noticed the tidiness of the room. How long had she been in there? The dishes were cleared away and the room was spotless. "Was housekeeping here?"

"Briefly. They'll be back later to tidy properly." He slipped the phone back into his pocket. "Ready?"

As she ever would be.

* * * *

The next few hours were spent exploring the lavish hotel. Alex was amazingly knowledgeable about nearly every aspect of the building, from the tiniest detail up to the overall vision of the rebuild. Watching him talk about his work and the passion he had for the hotel showed her a very different side of him.

This was the Alex who loved his work. Who never stopped thinking or looking for something new to invent or create. The Alex who was just emerging before he'd disappeared. The one she had fallen in love with.

It made the afternoon agony to get through. Maia focused on getting her notes and not finding a way of pressing herself up against him like she wanted to.

Outside, and staring at the magnificent building and the equally handsome man with new eyes, Maia felt herself falling in love with the hotel, the city, Alex…

"Maia?" Alex touched her arm, bringing her mind back to the present. "Is something wrong?" He stuck his cell phone back in his pocket.

She'd obviously missed a lot while she was staring. She shook her head. "I'm fine."

Alex didn't look so sure. "I've spoken with my father and he was delighted to hear that you're interested in seeing the new hotel. We can leave tonight."

"Great." That was a lot quicker than she'd anticipated. Then again, what did she expect? He didn't seem like the type of guy who would hang about if there was something he wanted. And Guillaume was their biggest cheerleader. He wouldn't stop them even if they were heading to nothing but a strip of sand in the ocean.

His eyebrows dropped together. "You don't sound so enthused. Is something wrong?"

"Not at all." Only that she was freaking out at the thought of traveling to an unknown location with Alex. Alone. Why did she have to be so eager to get the jump on everyone else? If she just took a second to think about things... That was the problem with just being around Alex. He made her lose her head.

She shrugged. "Maybe we should reschedule for another time. I have this article to finish and I haven't even spoken to Jo yet about your new hotel..."

Alex frowned, but it was quickly replaced with a cajoling smile. "Nonsense. I'm sure your editor will love getting the scoop on a new resort. And you'll have plenty of time once we're there to work on your article and polish it to perfection."

Maia couldn't think of an argument that would make a logical excuse not to go.

"Pack light. I'll pick you up in a couple of hours." He leveled his gaze at her. "Unless you think you need more time."

That would just give her more time to worry. "I just need my laptop and... What will I need?"

He grinned. "Just pack for a warm climate."

That was one mystery down. Maia pictured a tropical paradise with palm trees and crystalline water. Knowing Alex, he would have built paradise. But how would she get through the trip without going crazy?

Chapter Eight

By the time the helicopter dipped to land on a tiny patch of land, the fatigue of the twelve-hour flight had started to get to her. But the sight of the four villas situated on opposite ends of the little island perked her up considerably. It was a brilliant idea. Small. Quiet. Intimate. Perfect.

"Like what you see?"

Maia grinned, unable to hide her enthusiasm. "It's gorgeous."

His smile matched hers. "Wait until you get down there."

A small retinue of porters greeted them at the helipad and escorted them to a villa that perched on the water at the end of a long jetty.

The villa was opened with a smile and a bow.

What she saw inside took her breath away.

It was luxurious and tastefully decorated with local flair. Wood was the hero of the décor. It was everywhere. From the woven ceiling to the walls and floors. The natural grain gave the illusion of being inside a little indigenous hut while the furniture and amenities remained the height of luxury. The result was fantastic. Like being in a decadent dream world.

Maia rounded the room, taking everything in. The living area was sumptuously decorated with a couch that beckoned them to lounge on it. There was a dining area but, curiously, nothing resembling a kitchen or sleeping area.

When she turned to Alex, she could tell from the smile on his face that he knew what she was thinking. "Follow me."

Behind the couch was a staircase that led to an area that was situated under the patio out back.

Maia's eyes widened with every step.

The bedroom was dominated by a huge, lux bed, but the thing that made her jaw drop was the entire room, save for the wall the bed rested against, which was encircled by glass. Maia marveled at the ocean life around them. The dimming sunlight from above turned the water a dark sapphire, but she could still see the colorful coral reaching into the water. Schools of rainbow-hued fish darted about seemingly as curious about Maia and Alex as they were about them. It was magnificent. She could only imagine what it would look like out there in the light of day.

"So what do you think?"

As if he couldn't tell from the way her jaw was hanging that she loved everything about this place. "I still don't see a kitchen," she teased with a smile.

"That's because we have a world-renowned chef on the island who will prepare you what you like according to a questionnaire I took the liberty of filling out for the both of us. He will judge our tastes and create meals specifically for us."

That was amazing. "And he's been sitting around waiting for us? I thought this place wasn't open yet."

"I wanted you to have the full experience, so while this is the only villa running right now, we will have every luxury that will be at our guests' disposal." He chuckled. "If you're worried about putting them out, don't be. They are getting fully compensated for their time and effort."

That wasn't exactly what she was thinking. As much as she didn't like the idea of people just sitting around waiting to do stuff for her, Maia was more worried about what it was going to be like to have to leave this place when it was all over.

"Wait a second. This is the only villa running?" Her heart started to flutter.

"Yes, I thought that having two running just for us would be a waste." Alex stepped closer but stopped just a hair's breadth from her. "Don't worry. I'll take the couch."

It made her feel a little better, but she was afraid that the longer she spent here, the less time he'd be spending on that couch. And that he'd engineered it that way.

His phone buzzed and, with a quick glance, he smiled. "The chef has prepared a light meal to welcome us." Alex let his eyes wander over her fatigued form. "Unless you'd rather skip it and go straight to bed."

She knew what he meant and that it wasn't supposed to be as suggestive as it sounded, but her stomach flipped just the same. "It would be a shame to let good food go to waste."

His smile tilted in amusement. "Indeed."

Alex let her go up the stairs first but once she got to the top, there was nothing around that indicated there was food about.

"Head outside. Back to the beach. To your right."

She didn't have to see him to know that he was smiling.

Maia did as she was told and was grinning with delight even before she reached the beach.

A decadent picnic was set up that looked like something out of the *Arabian Nights*. Candles flickered in colored glasses spread out over the sand. They converged on a simple gazebo with a palm roof sparkling with white lights and gossamer curtains that billowed in the sweetly fragrant breeze. On the sand within there was a triangular blanket that was held in place with more candles, the largest of which was in the middle at the center of a spread of finger food all carefully covered with little nets. An ice bucket and two champagne flutes glittered in the flickering light. Brightly colored pillows marked their seats, which Maia took without a second thought.

She curled her legs under her and inhaled deeply. The air there was fresh, salted with the sea, perfumed with exotic flowers and spiced with the food laid out before them. The ambience was different from the sultry, hectic city vibe of Nice. As far as she was concerned, it was perfect.

Alex sat next to her, leaning on one elbow, a knee angled toward the star-sprinkled sky. He lifted the nets one by one revealing plates that looked more like art than something to be eaten. Everything she could see was mouth-watering. How did he know what to pick? They hadn't eaten together often enough for him to know what she preferred…

He picked up a skewer laden with plump grilled prawns. "Enjoy. You must be hungry."

She was. Maia copied him because the prawns looked amazing and quickly followed up with a glistening chicken wing that was coated in something both sweet and fiery.

Not much was said during their meal. She got the impression that he was as starving as she was. It didn't take them long to decimate the food and empty half the bottle of champagne.

"Feeling better?" Alex sipped the last of his drink and put the glittering glass down.

"Much." All she needed now was a good night's sleep, but how could she when her mind was buzzing about the possibilities that the following day brought? "What's on the agenda for tomorrow?"

"I thought I would give you a glimpse of what lovers would have to expect when coming to visit the island."

Her pulse flared. "Really? So what would that entail?"

"A slice of island life. More good food. Exploring ruins in Belize. Massages. Diving. Lounging." He caught her eye. "Anything you want to do."

Being so close to him made Maia want to do a lot of things. None of which she was going to allow herself.

"Right now I just want to try out that bed." Maia realized just how suggestive it sounded the moment the words left her lips. She clamped her mouth shut in an attempt not to further embarrass herself.

He said nothing as he stood up. Alex reached out a hand and helped her to her feet. He refused to let go. Instead, he linked their fingers together as they quietly made their way back to the villa.

It would have been so easy for her to fall under the spell of the island and truly believe that they were a pair of vacationing lovers looking for time away together.

Maia snapped herself out of it. She was there to do a job. For her career. Her long-ignored libido could just stay out of it. Only, with Alex holding her hand and the magic of the island, it was giving her a serious punch to the gut, reminding her just how long it had been since she'd been with a man. With Alex.

The moment they reached the door, she pulled her hand out of his grasp. "I'll see you in the morning." She gave him what felt even to her like a weak smile and darted down to the bedroom.

It didn't take her long to find the controls to the windows. The smart glass instantly fogged ensuring her privacy, not that she had anything to worry about besides the fish.

Too tired to go looking through her suitcase for her clothes, Maia stripped down to her underwear and fell into the heavenly softness of the bed.

Alex flipped onto his side, cursing the length of the couch. There was no way he would be able to fit himself comfortably on it. He envisioned Maia in the luxurious bed just a few steps below and groaned. He couldn't imagine what she would do if he tried to get in it with her. Persuading her wouldn't be a hardship, if she didn't try to kill him in the attempt. In fact, he rather liked the idea of kissing her into submission. Caressing that smooth, pale skin and watching it turn rosy with passion…

But he refused to give in to the temptation. Alex knew that she was attracted to him. He could feel the frisson of awareness that hummed between them. He saw it in her eyes. He would simply take his time and when she came to him, it would be that much better.

When he rolled again, the rigid state of his body reminded him that patience wasn't a virtue at the moment.

Giving up on the couch, he got up, took the pillow and sheet with him and went to the back patio. The huge net suspended like a hammock over the water was his only other bet to getting any sleep unless he wanted to stretch out on the deck. He rolled onto it and made himself comfortable. As far as beds went, it was great. Fresh air, the soothing sound of the waves, it was perfect.

So why couldn't he stop thinking about Maia and get to sleep? Because he had made the mistake of imagining her naked and spread beneath him, that's why. He tried to distract himself by shifting his train of thought elsewhere to something, anything, other than Maia. Unfortunately for him, his thoughts always circled back.

What had she been like nearly a decade ago? She would have been, what? In her late teens? Imagining Maia as a bright-eyed youth, unjaded and looking forward to the future made him flinch. Had he truly been the one to turn her into who she was now? Not that she wasn't still stunning and smart. But Maia was guarded, closed off by walls of ice. He wanted to be the one to break down those barriers.

But if he was the one who had hurt her, as he was beginning to believe, did he have a chance?

Chapter Nine

The sunlight filtered into the room, waking Maia. She immediately scrambled out of bed to press the button to clear the glass. Just as she suspected, the scene was even more stunning in daylight. The colors of the fish and coral were even more vibrant now and she could see further into the clear water. It was definitely something she could get used to waking up to every morning.

She stood marveling at the sight for a while only to be disturbed when a chiseled male body splashed into the water above and began cutting through it with sure strokes.

Alex wore black shorts and goggles. The rest of his glorious body was bare for her to study unabashedly. Long and lean, his powerful form easily ate up the distance and with a deft flip, he headed back toward the villa.

Maia watched mesmerized as he did this half a dozen times without slowing his pace. On his final return to the villa, he stopped and dove into the coral. He watched the fish, drifting among them like he belonged there. It wasn't long before his gaze followed a school of silver fish zipping past the window and saw her. He cocked his head and grinned, watching her a moment longer before resurfacing.

She looked down at herself and groaned. She'd totally forgotten that she was only in her underwear. Maia blindly gathered an outfit to wear for the day and headed straight upstairs to the bathroom.

After an extra-long shower, she got dressed, did her hair and lightly applied makeup. Maia glared at her reflection. She'd stalled long enough. She couldn't even make up the excuse to change because the dress she'd grabbed was perfect for a day on the island, provided they weren't going spelunking or anything of the sort, of course.

Alex sat at a tiny table set up on the patio, reading a paper and drinking coffee in nothing but his shorts. She'd taken up the one bathroom so he hadn't had a chance to wash the sea off him. And now she was forced to have breakfast while staring at his bare chest. Something that obviously bothered her way more than it did him from the looks of it.

He stood with a smile when he saw her. "Good morning. I trust you had a pleasant sleep."

"Wonderful." She slid into the seat he pulled out for her and stared at her plate and the artfully carved fruit displayed upon it. Perfect, again. Maia speared the fruit and did her best to keep her eyes on her food. She began to relax cell by cell as they enjoyed the morning sunlight in mutual silence.

As she sipped her coffee, Alex plucked a slice of mango from her plate. "I thought that today we would explore the jungle. There are some ruins that might interest you."

So she'd chosen the wrong outfit after all. "That sounds good."

"Excellent." He put down the paper, his eyes instantly catching hers. Alex looked like there was something on the tip of his tongue, but he smiled, said, "*Bon appétit*," and dug into his meal.

Maia did the same. "What ruins are there to see?" She'd always had a fascination with archeology and the thought of being able to see ruins that she hadn't before made her skin tingle. Or it could have been the man across the table from her? No. Definitely the thought of exploring ruins.

"I thought we'd visit Caracol first. It's supposed to be the most important archeological site in the area. Have you heard of it?"

Maia shook her head.

"I've visited only once when we were scouting the area. I don't think you will be disappointed."

Fascinated, Maia smiled at him. "What can you tell me about it?"

He put down his fork and a small smile curved his lips. "If I remember correctly, it's thought to have been occupied in 1200 BCE and covers approximately two hundred square kilometers. There are a great number of structures that I think we'll enjoy exploring. There is a team investigating the area right now that will be able to help us learn more.

Just from that tiny titbit of information, Maia buzzed with excitement and her food was forgotten. "Just let me get changed and I'll be ready to go whenever you are."

"I'll just get showered." Alex stood and Maia couldn't look away from the taut expanse of skin and light sprinkling of hair on his chest. "Be right back."

"Uh-huh. I mean, of course. I'll just get changed." Maia stumbled on the leg of the chair, but she waved him away when he tried to help her steady herself. "I'll be right back too."

It wasn't until she was back in the bedroom that she was able to breathe again. What was that? Since when did she ever get tongue-tied and clumsy? She rubbed her forehead as she mentally sorted through her clothes for something suitable to wear.

Thanks to her need to be prepared for any occasion, she had jeans, hiking boots, and a T-shirt with her. Minutes later, she was on the jetty with her camera and notepad all slung in a bag over her shoulder.

Alex emerged dressed in khakis and white button-down shirt and was just finishing up yet another call. He pointed to the phone. "The guide will meet us at the helipad on the other side."

"Great. Are you ready?"

He grinned. "Always."

* * * *

The helicopter trip was a blur of blue from above and below until they reached the mainland and the dense vegetation of the jungle turned the scene beneath a dark green.

As promised, a jovial little man met them on the other side. Alex informed her on the way over that he was the head of a team of archeologists currently digging there and was considered the foremost expert on the ruins.

Who else would the Girards find but the best?

They chatted on the quick Jeep ride over about what they would see but Maia wasn't prepared for the sheer magnificence of what they encountered.

The moment she walked across the grassy ground to look up at the towering ruins, Maia felt a mix of awe and humility. She immediately pulled out her camera and started snapping. The information that the guide gave them was noted as they followed him around.

The blazing sun beat down on the stones, and she marveled at how long it must have done this very thing and how much longer it would go on doing so. It was mind-boggling that something created by man had lasted so many millennia.

Alex seemed to share her drive to climb every step and explore every crevice in the city and they even managed to outlast their guide, who was happy to give them pertinent information before they explored the last few buildings.

The sun hung low on its descent as they climbed the last structure. The steep steps were hard on her legs after a day of scaling just about everything she could find a stable foothold. As if sensing her fatigue, Alex took her hand and led the way up the remaining steps. Once they stood at the summit, Maia gazed out at the ruins and wondered what they had looked like when they were shiny and new.

"Magnificent, isn't it?" Alex handed her his canteen of water.

Maia took it gratefully and took a few sips. "Very. It's incredible what they were able to achieve."

She handed it back. Maia wasn't ready for the zap when his hand grazed hers. Biting her bottom lip, she tried to pull hers from his grasp, but he tangled his fingers with hers. Maia couldn't look away from Alex.

His mesmerizing gaze held hers and Maia's body responded. All the aches she felt previously disappeared except for the one growing low in her belly.

"Um. Thanks." She forced herself to look away, shattering the moment. Maia turned her gaze to the stone glowing in the dimming light.

He took it from her. "You're welcome."

"I think we've seen just about everything, haven't we?"

"If you are happy to leave, we will."

Nodding, she took a few more photos and started her descent, carefully avoiding the hand he offered her.

Maia dazedly made her way down. It was getting too easy to be with Alex. She had facts oozing out of her ears and two memory cards full of photos and while she wanted to see more, what she was most interested in was time with him.

The thought did occur to her to ask to camp out with the archeologists. She wanted to learn as much as she could about the site and at the same time it would keep her from an all too intimate situation with Alex. But they'd already taken up enough of their time. So with a promise to add pictures of the ruins to her article to raise awareness of what they were doing, she bade them goodbye.

Alex was silent the whole ride back. He'd been quiet most of the day. He'd asked questions and added to discussions here and there. He'd actually been quite knowledgeable about the history of the area. But for the most part, he was happy just soaking everything in. Quite unlike what she'd expected from him.

Not that anything she'd expected of him had come to fruition. Apart from the vile things he'd said to her after she'd thrown the champagne at him, he was a good man. He had a tendency to be a bit distant, but over the past few days, he'd opened up a little.

She beamed. So had she.

Maybe his father was right. They were good for each other.

"You look content." Alex had angled his head to look at her as they walked back to the villa.

She gazed up at him. "I had a great day."

"Glad to hear it. But it's not over yet. I'm sure the chef has something spectacular planned for dinner."

Her grin widened.

And he was right. The patio was decorated with strings of lights and a large table was set with candles, gilded plates and gleaming silverware. The enormous lobster drew her eyes so she barely noticed anything else on the table.

"I have to admit I took a guess with this one. It's one of my favorites. I hope that it doesn't disappoint."

She knew he loved lobster. It was one of the things they had in common, but, of course, he couldn't remember that. Maia shook her head. "Not at all."

He pulled her chair out for her before pouring the wine. Alex briskly served her and sat back.

Maia couldn't wait to dive in, but Alex hadn't made a move toward the food. "Aren't you having any?"

"I will. I just want to see if you like it."

She bit her lip. "Why? What have you done to it?" Maia joked.

He chuckled. "Of course I didn't do anything to the food. I just want to see if you enjoy my favorite meal as much as I do."

A smiled curved her lips as she speared a succulent bit of lobster. "It's my favorite as well."

A grin lit up his face, making him look like the Alex that she remembered. "It seems that we have a lot in common." He took his share of the food and dove in.

She scoffed. "I don't think enjoying similar food can be counted for a lot."

He lifted his eyebrows. "There's the archeology as well. I bet if we sat down and actually had a conversation, we would find a few more."

That depended on what he wanted to talk about. The last thing she wanted to discuss was their past. She just wanted to forget about it and move on. But she knew what Alex was like and he wouldn't be satisfied until he uncovered everything.

"You look pensive." Alex chewed thoughtfully as he regarded her.

"Not really. Just tired I guess. And I still have a lot of work to get done."

"Of course. Perhaps we should take it easy tomorrow then, give you a chance to catch up."

There was still so much to see and do. She wanted the article to cover everything. "I can manage."

The smile on his face was soft. "Are you in that much of a hurry to get away from me?"

That gave her pause. Maia was surprised that she actually wanted the opposite. She wanted to get to know him. She knew the plan was to get the job done and get out. Now, she realized that the man that he'd become was fascinatingly different from the boy she'd known. She wanted to delve deeper into who he was now. Find out what made him smile, his interests. Just to spend time with him.

"I'll take that as a yes, then." He shifted back in his seat and took a long sip of wine.

"Not at all." Her eyes met his fleetingly before dropping to her own drink. "Spending time with you hasn't been all bad."

He chuckled before a warm hand closed around hers. The jolt she got from his touch lifted her eyes to meet his smoldering gaze. "I could say the same thing."

Her mind faltered on what to say, what to do next. He didn't seem to have the same problem and lifted her hand to his lips so he could gently kiss her knuckles. "Tomorrow we will take it a bit slower. I'll find us something to do that won't have you out for the entire day. It might be nice to spend some time here. Together."

And alone.

Maia appreciated that he was thinking about her needs. At least that part of him hadn't changed. She knew that they were pretty much alone on the island. She just wasn't sure how great an idea it would be to be alone so isolated with her defenses falling rapidly as they were. At least when they were out doing things, there were other people around. Plenty of distractions. The thought of spending a lot of time at the villa alone made her feel vulnerable.

"You don't seem pleased with that idea." Alex watched her intently and could probably glean everything that was going on in her head.

She quickly shook it off and smiled at him. "So what else is there to do here?"

The curve of his lips never wavered. "So much. But I think we need to pace ourselves. I don't want to wear you out."

Thoughts of how he could wear her out sent a blast of heat to her cheeks and started her heart racing. If he could do that with just a few words and a touch, what could he do when he really wanted to?

She delicately pulled her hand from his grasp. "Don't worry about me. I'm sure I can handle whatever you throw at me."

Alex smirked. "Oh, I have no doubt."

Chapter Ten

Alex must have taken her remark as a challenge. The next day he had a long list of things to see and do. Starting immediately after a light breakfast, they walked to the opposite side of the island to go snorkeling.

Maia had traveled all over the globe and swum in some of the most amazing waters, but this one was pure magic. The morning light filtered through the water to play with the corals and the fish darting through it, giving it an almost otherworldly appearance.

Alex tirelessly led her to one amazing spot after another. At one point, they were even joined by a curious turtle that swam alongside them for a time.

Maia broke through the surface with a smile on her face. Pulling out the snorkel, she flipped onto her back and let the sun warm her skin.

Alex wasn't too far behind. He greeted her with a laugh. "You look right at home."

"I've always felt at home in the water but this was absolutely incredible. I wish I could stay forever."

He made a sound that gave her the impression that he felt the same. "I'm sure the owner could make a villa free for you whenever you like."

It was on the tip of her tongue to accept. Who wouldn't? "I might have to take you up on that offer sometime." She said the words, even though she had no intention of taking advantage of him or his connections.

She felt a hand close around hers and the next thing she knew, she was vertical and in his arms. "Alex—"

He silenced her with a kiss. Slanting over her mouth, he stole her breath away with his intensity. When she parted her lips to draw more air, he delved deeper, his tongue caressing hers. He slowly slid his hands up her body to hold her steady against his sensual onslaught.

Maia pulled him closer, loving the sensation of his body so tight against hers. He was solid. All hard muscle and angles. It was wonderful to feel him against her again. But gone was the boy she remembered. This Alex might have smelled and tasted familiar, but that was where the similarities ended. He turned her nerveless with nothing more than his lips and hands. She was dimly aware of one hand gliding down her body to cup her bottom and hold her against his impressive erection. When Alex pulled back, it took a moment for her eyes to refocus.

His smile was triumphant. "I've never met anyone who calls to me as you do."

His words only reminded her that he didn't remember her and the pain that came with the fact. With a well-placed shove, she put space between them. "Alex, please…"

His eyes darkened and his hands closed around her hips to pull her back toward him. "There's something about you, Maia, it draws me." His gaze snared hers. "I know you feel it too."

"Alex. We can't." The words were weak on her lips.

"We can." He plundered her mouth again in an almost successful attempt at wiping all thoughts from her mind.

For a long moment she could do nothing but let him. Not that she didn't enjoy every second of it. It just brought back bad memories that she couldn't deal with right then. She braced her hands on his shoulders and she knew he had let her push him back. "Alex…"

"Maia, I'm not going to say I'm sorry for that. I find you intriguing and I want to learn more about you. Everything."

That was what Maia was afraid of.

Alex didn't know what came over him, but in that moment he had to feel her against him. He had to kiss her. And when she responded to him as she did, he knew that she felt the chemistry between them as well. It was combustible. What started as a little experiment to gauge her response turned into something infinitely more.

Alex had half hoped that something in his memory would click. Instead, nothing but lust, pure and molten, blasted through him.

He'd known kissing her would be delicious, but he'd had no idea that a simple kiss would affect him so much. She was dangerously addictive. Did he want to get hooked? Absolutely. But he had to keep his head if he was going to find out more about her. Rushing into things was a sure-fire way to push her away. But damned if he didn't want to shove clothing aside and take her right there in the ocean.

He watched her try to compose herself and put the icy mask façade back in place. Only this time she seemed unable to do so completely. It made her even more attractive to know that he affected her as much as she did him.

What he wanted was to get to the real her, the one who wouldn't hide behind excuses about work and cool professionalism. He'd seen a glimpse of the woman beneath and knew he only wanted more.

He would bide his time. At least until his control frayed to the point of snapping.

* * * *

Maia spent the rest of the day in a distracted daze. She dutifully took note of the quality of the service, details about their surroundings. Thankfully, she had her camera and her phone to dictate notes to or else she'd never remember any of it.

Alex was the perfect host, introducing her to people, showing her noteworthy locations, filling her in on interesting facts and behind the scenes information. If only she hadn't been so unfocused.

Alex must have noticed her state of distraction because he'd backed off a little. Giving her the space she needed. But Maia could tell that it only piqued his interest even more.

Damn the man's inquisitive nature.

Maia could only hope that his attention would be directed elsewhere. And soon.

Before long, she found herself sitting at their table overlooking the water with yet another sumptuous meal laid out beautifully before her.

"Maia? Has the magic of the island been lost on you?" Alex watched her closely and she hadn't even noticed.

"Not at all." She forced herself to smile and made a show of studying the meal. "This looks wonderful.

He put his hand on hers, stopping her from fidgeting with the napkin. "Your mind has been elsewhere most of the day. Is something wrong?"

"Not at all."

He picked up his wine and regarded her silently for a long moment. "You seem a little...off."

She smiled weakly. "Sorry. I guess I have a lot on my mind."

"Anything I can help with?"

She smiled gratefully. He was always so considerate. "Thanks, but no. Besides I'm sure you've got enough on your plate."

He squeezed her hand. "If you can think of anything I can do, let me know."

She knew he meant it. "I will. Thanks."

With a smile, he let go of her hand so they could both start eating. "*Bon appétit.*"

"So what do you think of the resort so far?"

Maia shrugged. "What can I say? It's wonderful. It's definitely unique."

He grinned, relaxing completely for the first time since Nice. "I'm glad you think so."

She picked at her food for a moment as she eyed him. Alex patiently watched her.

"You're expecting a 'but'."

"Of course I am. Someone who has traveled as you have must have some critiques."

Thinking over what they had seen and done as well as her overall impression of the island, there weren't many things she could fault. "I can't think of anything, really." She speared a baby carrot and chewed it thoughtfully. "What happens when there's bad weather?"

Challenged, he leaned forward and linked his fingers together. "Depending on the situation, there are evacuation plans. A helicopter can be here within minutes to take everyone off the island."

"And if that's not a possibility?"

"A ferry is ready if the weather prevents air evacuation. If neither are viable, the villas are strong, well built. They can withstand a lot. But if they are stressed beyond their limits, there is an underground bunker at the center of the island."

Satisfied with his answer, she nodded in admiration. "It seems you've thought of everything."

"I hope I have. I want this to be a destination for couples to relax and enjoy themselves."

"Well, it's certainly incredible. I can't say I've ever been anywhere like it before." Maia smiled at him. "I think you have a winner on your hands."

Alex grinned hugely. "I'm glad. I've put a lot of myself into this place." He glanced around, a delighted smile on his lips.

"I can see that. You've done an amazing job, Alex." She was proud of him and what he had accomplished. The resort was destined to be a hit.

"Thank you." He openly studied her. Just as she was beginning to squirm under his gaze, he said, "We need to celebrate."

Was he kidding? *Celebrate how? Why?* Just because she thought the resort would be a hit? But before she could reply, he stood and was around the table, scooping her up into his arms.

His smile and laughter were infectious and she found herself joining in. For an instant, she forgot about everything. The world dropped away and they were just two people enjoying the moment. And it felt wonderful. More than.

Alex spun her around and lowered his face to her throat where he muttered something she didn't catch.

"What was that?" Her mind was already on meltdown from being held by him.

His lips grazed her neck on the way up to nibble on her earlobe. His breath caressed the path his lips took. "I said, I don't know what it is about you but you make me feel…"

She craned her neck to look at him. "Feel what?"

Maia couldn't decipher the look he gave her and all attempts were blasted away when his lips found hers.

No one could kiss like Alex. No one could make her breathless and dizzy, or make her heart slam against her ribcage like he did. She couldn't stop her arms from winding around his neck or her hands from tangling in his hair.

Alex groaned and deepened the kiss, dueling her tongue with his. When his arms banded around her and crushed her against him, Maia let herself get swept up into his embrace. It felt too good to be against his hard body. To feel him against her.

The rush of sensation was heady but not totally unexpected. Maia knew in the back of her mind that it would be like this, but she wasn't ready for how easily he tore through her defenses and left her trembling.

Alex didn't give her a chance to breathe, let alone think. All she could do was feel and she wanted more. More sensation. More Alex. Maia had spent too long closed behind icy walls but she knew that it was only with Alex that she felt this way. That she could even feel this way again.

Maia wound herself around him, needing as much contact as she could get.

With a groan, Alex cradled her closer. "I need to know that this is what you want. Say the word and we'll stop."

She tangled her fingers in his hair as she gazed into his eyes and dragged him back down for another searing kiss.

When she opened her eyes again, they had somehow managed to make it to the bedroom.

Alex gently placed her at the center of the bed and made quick work of her clothing, peeling, tugging and tossing with clear and definite purpose. When she was bare to him, he blazed a trail over her skin with his hands, followed by his mouth and tongue.

Maia writhed beneath him, clawing at his clothes, needing to feel his skin against hers. Buttons pinged across the room in her impatience to run her hands over the hard muscles hidden beneath. The groan she was rewarded with when she raked her nails over his solid shoulders made her smile.

He still liked it.

Alex didn't know what it was about her, but he couldn't get enough of Maia. Every sigh and moan just made him want more. He craved her. Needed her like he needed his next breath.

For a man who prided himself on self-control and never letting anything get under his skin, she was doing an admirable job of proving that belief to be utterly wrong.

When she'd thrown the drink at him in the restaurant, he was sure that she was either insane or incredibly skilled at getting what she wanted. He'd never had a woman attack him as an opening salvo. Then the story of how he'd abandoned her made him suspicious again. But nothing she had told him seemed to be a lie. The more he got to know her, the more he fell under her spell. He just felt that there was something he was missing. Something she wasn't telling him.

Alex knew that he was gaining her trust and it was paramount if she was going to open up to him. And he wanted to know everything about her, including what he had done to shatter her trust in men. He needed to know so he could make it right.

He hadn't planned on her charming him so completely. Even now, he knew he should stop. That he should have never brought her here of all places. But he couldn't help himself.

Maia was an addiction that was overtaking his consciousness and there wasn't anything he wanted to do to change that.

Alex hooked his hands around her hips and dragged her forward so he could claim her lips again. She tasted of sunshine and something that was intrinsically Maia that he found absolutely intoxicating.

He let his hands explore the skin he'd been wanting to see and touch and taste for days. Alex wanted Maia like he had never wanted anyone else. She was a compulsion. A burning obsession. She made him forget all his rules and made him truly feel for the first time in a very long time.

And he would have her.

Maia tunneled a hand through his hair to anchor him against her when he dragged his lips downward to nip at her throat. But that didn't stop him from slowly moving lower. Over her collarbone, licking the valley between her breasts, before taking one peak into his hot mouth. She couldn't stop the groan that climbed her throat. Arching against him, she sighed when he moved to circle the other with his tongue.

When she was sure she was going to black out, his hands joined in. Gliding down her side, he stopped one at her breast to cup and caress while the other traveled lower. Down her side, teasing over her belly then over her thigh. She parted them for him only caring about feeling more of his touch. To feel Alex again.

He leaned back a little to look into her eyes as he pushed his fingers into her wet heat. She bit back a scream when he slid them in, driving her pleasure higher and higher. But just as she was about to have the fastest orgasm of her life, he pulled away.

Maia clawed at him. "Alex. Please."

He kissed her again, shifting their positions so that he was between her thighs. Alex nipped her ear as he whispered, "I want to be deep inside you when you climax. I want to feel you around me."

He swiftly took care of protection before he lowered himself down to her.

His words alone were enough to make her eyes roll heavenward. So close. Maia was sure he could tell just how close she was and that he barely had to do a thing to get her there. Not to be outdone, she ran the back of her fingers down the ridges of his abdomen, slowly making her way to torture him as he had her.

Divining her intent, he snatched her hand away and imprisoned them both over her head in one hand. The movement wedged himself against her. The slightest shift of his hips and he would slip inside. "I don't think so."

"Then stop tormenting me." Maia hooked a leg around his hip and dragged him closer, impaling herself with him.

Not letting her control the speed of his descent, he slid forward slowly, deliciously, filling her with an almost leisurely stroke.

The feel of his hard body against her, within her, was better than she remembered. When he reached bottom, it made her breath hitch. Alex held still for a breath and just stared into her eyes while he gave her a long moment for her body to adjust to his size.

Stretched to her limits she circled her hips, wrapping her legs around his, letting him know in no uncertain terms that she wanted him to move.

Alex's groan as he pulled out and pushed back into her caused a wicked little smile to curve her lips. She had little chance to revel in her newfound power as his thrusts grew deeper, robbing her of coherent thought. All she could do was react, feel—revel—as her body tightened again.

Alex plunged into her, thrusting deeply, pulling almost all the way out and pushing his girth into her again and again. The friction of his huge, veined erection against her sensitized flesh as he pumped into her raised goosebumps on her skin. His ragged breath mingled with hers as they strained against each other, each pushing the other ever closer to the precipice.

For a second Maia hung there, right at the edge. Alex lifted his head to capture and hold her gaze as, with a heavy thrust, he took her over. Maia exploded with a keening cry, convulsing around him and arching into him.

Alex's sexy smile as he thrust, drawing out her orgasm, turned into an expression of pure ecstasy as he joined her moments later with a shout.

He dropped his head to her shoulder, his thrusts slow to draw out his own pleasure. Eventually, he dropped, completely spent. For a long while, they lay blissfully entwined. His gaze lifted to hers and, for an instant, Maia thought she saw a spark of recognition there before he blinked and it was gone.

Alex pulled her with him as he rolled to his side. Sighing, he stretched. "That was incredible."

Maia couldn't help the smile that his words brought to her lips. He was even better than she remembered. But of course he was. He'd only just been figuring out how potent he was sexually when they'd been together.

He had been amazing then. Now he was spectacular.

And now, he definitely knew how to use it.

Just imagining how many women got to know this fact about him made her chest ache a little. It had been a long time apart, so he didn't have the memories of her that she had of him, and she needed to remember that.

"Hey. What's wrong?" He twisted so that she was on top of him. He wrapped his arms around her waist, holding her tightly against him, his nose inches away from hers as he searched her eyes. "You just checked out on me."

Her head was chaotic with memories, old and new colliding with what she thought she knew about him and what she actually knew now. It was a confusing mess. "I just need a moment."

"Maia. I know you're keeping something from me."

She tried to respond but he cut her off.

"I hope that you will learn to open up to me because I have no intention of letting you go."

"Letting me go?" The sheer arrogance of his words grated at her. Strung tight as they were, she lashed out, shoving at his chest. "You have some nerve."

He stared at her with genuine confusion. "What's the matter?"

"You! That's what's the matter. You bring me here under the guise of showing me your new resort and it was all just to seduce me. Admit it!" And she'd served herself up to him on a plate.

Maia grabbed the sheets and wrapped them around herself as she searched for something to wear.

Alex was visibly baffled as he slid off the bed to stand completely, magnificently, naked to face her. "Calm down. Where is this coming from? We've had an amazing few days and just had fantastic sex. And all of a sudden you're going crazy."

She glared at him. "So now I'm crazy?"

Alex stared acerbically at her sheet-covered form. "What would you call this?"

He had a point. But what could she say? That she'd thought of him with other women and that it enraged and sickened her? That the sex with him was incredible and that frightened the life out of her?

He didn't give her a chance to come up with anything. "I know you have trouble with intimacy and I can handle that. I think we both realize what we have here is special."

Of course she knew. It was the second time she'd found it with him.

"Please." Alex wound his arms around her, his breath warm on her ear. "Come back to bed."

She opened her mouth to apologize but he hushed her with a gentle finger on her lips.

Maia let him lead her back to bed. Alex slid in behind her, peeled away the sheet and wrapped himself around her in its place.

For a long while, he simply held her, letting his warmth and strength seep into her. And Maia did find comfort in being skin to skin with him. Feeling his steady heart beat against her back, hearing his breath, was incredibly soothing. Cell by cell, Maia's muscles unbunched until she was pliant as he began to explore her again.

He glided his hands slowly over her skin in slow, mesmerizing strokes. He caressed her skin with the downward drag of the backs of his fingers. Alex brushed her hair away to nip the skin just below her ear. "You are beautiful."

Giving in to the urge to lean into his touch, she shimmied against him. Loving the feel of his hard body and hair-roughened skin against her. She craned her head back to look at him. He was easily the most handsome man she'd ever seen. His dark hair and eyes, classical features and a lush mouth made for sin. And his body...

"I want you again, Maia."

As if the erection prodding her in the back wasn't enough to tell her that much.

She twisted in his arms so she lay on her back under him. "It seems that's another thing we have in common."

Alex kissed her, deeply, coaxingly. Like she was air and he had been trapped in a vacuum. He skillfully, explored her mouth as he held her head in place with one hand while he plundered her mouth. The other hand, he used to explore.

He cupped a breast, flicking his thumb over her nipple before pinching it delicately. Maia reared up at the sensation, moaning into his mouth.

Everything he did added to the liquid ache growing deep inside her. He instinctively knew exactly how to touch her and where to fuel her excitement.

Alex took his time. He continued to kiss her as he dragged his hand lower to slip between her thighs. He circled her clit before delving deeper, first easing one finger then two into her wet slit.

He dipped them deep, crooking them on his way out. Slowly, he drew them back, using her own juices to lubricate his fingers as he renewed his attention on her swollen clit.

Maia mewled when he rubbed her gently, coaxing the most exquisite pleasure from her body.

She whispered against his lips, "Please, Alex."

He smiled and deftly took care of protection before he was over her again. Surging into her.

Maia met him thrust for thrust. The pleasure built on itself until she exploded once again with a gasp.

Alex slammed into her moments later, coming with a groan.

When she could finally focus her eyes once again, she stared up at him, knowing she was in danger of losing her heart to him once again.

Chapter Eleven

Maia could feel a difference in the air the moment she woke up. Before she even opened her eyes. The air was thick and hot. Humidity clung to the skin that was exposed above the tangle of sheets. The room was charged with electricity. And it had nothing to do with Alex.

Speaking of Alex, he was nowhere she could see. Not that she could see much of anything. The crystalline water that she'd gotten accustomed to waking to was dark. And a push of the button to clear her view didn't help her see anything in the seething water.

"Alex?" She hated to admit it but she would feel better if she knew where he was.

"I'm up here, Maia."

She wrapped the sheet around herself and padded up the stairs to find him pacing in nothing more than a low-slung pair of jeans in deep conversation on his phone.

His steps stalled a second as he took a moment to look at Maia. A slow smile spread over her lips as he waved at the coffee table where a small breakfast feast sat waiting for her. Coffee, fruit, croissants all beckoned.

She smiled her thanks and sat.

Alex winked. With the phone wedged between his ear and shoulder, he poured the coffee and placed it before her.

Maia took a sip and speared a mango cube. From his side of the conversation, it didn't sound good.

He finished it quickly and gave her a grim smile before pecking her on the cheek. "Morning." He slid onto the seat next to her and draped an arm around her shoulders as if it was something they did every morning.

"Hi." She chewed the delectable morsel of fruit. "So what's going on?"

"It looks like we might be stuck here a little longer than expected. There's a storm preventing us from leaving today." Alex took a sip of his coffee. "I hope that doesn't upset you."

It clearly didn't bother him too much.

She shrugged. "Don't you have work to get back to?"

"Nothing that I can't manage from here for the moment." He pointed at the satellite phone he had just been using. "You're welcome to use it for however long the battery lasts."

"Thanks." Maia couldn't help but notice how relaxed he was. Since meeting again, he seemed truly at peace. Even though they were apparently stuck, he was smiling, the crease between his eyebrows was gone, and she could just feel that the energy from him had changed. If she didn't know better, she would think that he was basking in the glow of an intimate vacation rather than being trapped by a storm.

"Do you think we'll be stuck here a long time?"

Alex shrugged. "Would that be so bad?"

Not if they spent all their time like they had the night before. The look in his eyes as he caught her gaze told her he was thinking the same thing. As much as she would love to forget that there was a world outside this place, Maia knew that the bubble would burst sometime. It was better not to live under any delusions.

She shook her head. "Not if it's only for a few days."

He sat back. "Is spending time with me so arduous?"

"Of course not. The last few days have been amazing. But we do have lives we have to get back to. And what about the staff who are stuck here as well?"

"They are safe and will be well compensated." He slipped a piece of mango between her lips. "Anything else?"

"Alex..." Maia took a long breath, biding her time as she chewed and swallowed the succulent fruit.

She didn't even know what she wanted to say. It was just reflex to say no, to try to put as much space between them as possible. But hadn't their time at the resort proved that they could be good together? Who wouldn't want to spend time away from the world in a beautiful place with a handsome man who could do the things to her that Alex did? Was she crazy fighting this? It was as though everything were trying to drive them together. Even Mother Nature was conspiring against her. Maia was tired of fighting herself.

"Yes?" He used his finger to lazily trace circles over her shoulder.

"It sounds wonderful."

The smile spread slowly over his lips. "I thought so too." Alex dragged her with him as he leaned back.

The wind roared past the windows, causing the villa to tremble with the force of it.

Maia shivered a little with it. "Are we going to be okay here?"

"We should be fine as long as it doesn't get any worse. The last weather update I received said that it was going to be nothing more than a few days of high winds and a little rain." He smiled impishly. "Just enough to keep us from leaving paradise for a while."

Maia had to laugh at that. "I never would have taken you for someone who skips out on work."

He shook his head. "I'm not. I can't actually remember the last time that I wasn't in a hotel for anything but business." Alex closed his eyes and let his head drop back on the couch, a broad smile on his lips. "This feels good."

She knew the feeling. "I suppose it is weird, isn't it? You'd think from the way we make our livings we'd be living the high life. It's an endless stream of traveling, exotic locales, beautiful hotels. But I can't remember the last time I just stopped and took a breath. Enjoyed myself instead of wondering about square footage of a room. Or if there's something interesting to see or do in the area."

The chuckled that rumbled through him made her smile. "I guess we're just a couple of workaholics."

Yet another thing they had in common.

She sat leaning against him for a long while. Just listening to the storm raging outside. Things couldn't have been more different on the inside of the villa. It was still. Tranquil. She knew he felt it too.

But the chemistry simmering between them hadn't changed. It crackled in the air. She only had to look at him to want him. Maia knew from the way his eyes had darkened that he wanted her too.

"How are we going to fill our time without work to do?" Maia twisted around to straddle his hips.

His hands instantly went to her waist, holding her still as he ground himself against her. "I can think of a few ways."

"Only a few?"

"Is that a challenge?"

"Maybe." She knew that he wasn't one to back down. Every obstacle was faced and summarily conquered. And that was when they were still at university. She could only imagine what he was capable of now. All Maia knew was that she wanted to find out.

She let the sheet drop a little and was rewarded with an even bigger smile. Alex glided his hands up her sides to cup her breasts, pushing them together as he buried his face between them.

When his hot mouth closed around the hard peak and his tongue joined in, Maia wouldn't have cared if the storm tore down the walls around them.

It wasn't until Alex groaned and carefully slid out from under her that she heard the insistent knocking at the door. She scrambled to cover herself as Alex made his way to the door. He turned to check that she was ready, but the smoldering look that he gave her as his eyes swept over her told Maia that he could still see parts of her that aroused his interest.

"I guess I'll go get dressed." She was already partway down the stairs when she heard him greet whoever it was brave enough to wander about.

It took a few minutes to find something suitable, but she was caught up watching the rain ripple on the darkened surface of the water as it rolled. The fish were pulled to and fro by the force of the waves. It mirrored what she felt like being around Alex again. She gravitated toward him unable to break free. Not that she wanted to.

She never imagined that she would see Alex again. And now she was stuck in paradise with him, almost content. She closed her eyes and pressed her head against the smooth, cool surface of the glass. Maia smiled to herself.

Familiar arms coiled around her. "Thinking about me, I hope."

Chuckling, she spun in his arms to hook hers around his neck. "I was, actually. I can't believe I'm this relaxed in the middle of a storm."

"I'm glad you have confidence in me and the villa to keep you safe." He dropped a kiss on her nose.

"So who was at the door?"

"The caretaker wanted to make sure we had emergency supplies. Just in case."

"That was thoughtful of him."

He gave her a sardonic arch of an eyebrow. "More like he can't afford to have the boss hurt in the storm."

She rolled her eyes at his jaded comment. He would have seen it too, if the lights hadn't chosen that moment to go out. The dim light coming in from the window gave the room an eerie blue-gray glow. At least it was enough to see by. Sort of.

"And not a moment too soon." He took her hand and led her back up the stairs.

Two large boxes sat on the floor of the living room.

"Shall we see what we've got?" Alex pushed them toward the couch with his foot and sat, tugging Maia to sit on his lap.

The first was filled with food. Fresh and packaged. Enough to last the week if they needed it to. Alex pulled a lantern out of the other and turned it on. There were three others as well as various sized glow sticks, extra blankets, first-aid kits, even an extra battery for the satellite phone. Digging further there was pretty much anything else they could need in any emergency.

Maia was impressed by the high-tech gear, but was a little disappointed that they wouldn't be living by candlelight for a little while. "I was expecting candles."

Alex reached in and pulled out a fist full of long, tapered candles. "It looks like they've thought of everything."

Maia grinned. She would have to mention the staff's attention to detail in her article. "I really shouldn't be having such a good time during a storm."

"That would make the two of us."

"So what can we do today?" The rain pounding the roof and battering the windows made sure that they wouldn't be venturing outside any time soon.

His chuckle rumbled through her. "I'm sure I will be able to think of something to help keep you occupied." Alex nuzzled the soft skin under her ear, pausing to nip her earlobe playfully.

Maia let her head fall to the side, giving him easier access, letting him do whatever he pleased. She readily let the haze of pleasure cloud her mind as he slid his hands over her skin.

A shrill ring from the satellite phone brought her back to reality.

Groaning, Alex shifted her in his lap so he could reach the table and retrieve the insistently ringing phone and growled into it. "This had better be good." His expression changed when he heard the voice on the other end. "Sorry, Papa. Yes, we're both fine."

She waved at Alex, indicating that she would leave. He shook his head, but she didn't want to intrude on the conversation. Besides, she wanted to primp a little.

After a brisk shower, she stared at her clothes and cursed herself for not bringing something sexier. How was she to know that she would need it? It wasn't as though she went prowling for men on her trips. She spent the majority of her time exploring, fact finding then writing everything down. Most of her clothing was either comfortable, functional or suitable for business meetings.

Maia slipped into a simple white maxi dress and left her hair loose and her face bare. As she made her way back up, Maia noticed that the floor above was deathly silent except for the wail of the wind outside. "Alex?"

She found him at the doors of the balcony that overlooked the water. His stormy gaze rivaled the tempest raging outside. "Alex? What's the matter?"

Dread crept along her skin as he ignored her and continued to stare. What had his father told him? Whatever it was, it had to have been awful.

She circled around to stand next to him. "What's wrong? Is your father okay?"

He looked at her then, his eyes desolate and filled with pain. "I want the truth when I ask you this."

Maia's stomach dropped, but she nodded. She knew what was coming. It was time they cleared the air and stopped pretending.

"When I returned here and had that accident... Did I leave you while you were pregnant?"

Chapter Twelve

She exhaled a slow, deflating breath. "Yes."

His jaw tightened and she could see his throat working as if he was having a hard time swallowing the information.

"I suppose you had people look into my story." Of course he would. Alex was careful. Meticulous.

His eyes scanned the ocean, searching. "You weren't exactly forthcoming. I needed confirmation that you weren't a liar." He clenched and unclenched his hands. "My father brought my things from school out of storage."

Her lips curved downward. "And now that you know everything?"

He turned to glare at her. "How can I know everything? Anything? I don't remember any of it! All there is are a handful of photos and a few notes…"

Maia fought to find her voice. "Most of the photos would have been on your phone."

He choked back a wry laugh. "The one that got destroyed in the accident."

She sighed. "The only number I had to contact you."

Alex pressed his forehead against the glass a moment before he spun and grabbed her by the shoulders. "Did I know? I must have if my father was able to figure it out from my things…"

She nodded as she remembered the awed joy her news had brought to his face. The optimistic plans they'd made…

"And you thought I abandoned you and our child." He dropped his head to hers. "No wonder you attacked me the way you did. I'd have done much worse." As if he had just realized what he was doing, he dropped his hands from her shoulders and stepped back. His voice was choked as he said, "But no one has mentioned you having a child."

Maia let her gaze fall from his as tears threatened to fill her eyes. "You weren't the only one involved in an accident." She would never forget how tired and sick she had been for the first couple of months, then he'd disappeared. Two months of worry on top of the pregnancy had taken its toll on her. On the fateful day, Maia had passed out and fallen down a flight of stairs. She had been nearly four months along at the time. "I wasn't as careful as I should have been. I didn't take care of myself and paid the price for it."

"*Mon Dieu*," he muttered. Alex sounded utterly devastated as he gripped her to him. "You suffered so much alone."

"It was a long time ago." Maybe for her, but she could see the pain he was in. For him it had to be as though he'd just taken a knife in the chest.

"And I can remember nothing of it! Nothing of us!" Alex let Maia go and prowled a line between her and the window. "The things I accused you of being. How will you forgive any of it?"

"This is why I didn't want you to find out. It's in the past. There's nothing you can do about it now."

His burning gaze pinned her. "How can you be so forgiving?"

"It obviously didn't come overnight." Maia stepped in his path and cupped his cheeks with her hands, making sure that he looked her in the eyes. "It wasn't your fault. I understand that now and so should you."

"I'm so sorry." Alex closed his eyes briefly before opening them to search hers. "Will you tell me everything about our time together?"

The thought of having to walk him through what they'd had like he was an innocent bystander made her chest ache. "Can you answer a question first?"

"Anything."

"I tried for months to contact you after you left. To find out why you hadn't come back. To find out if you were okay." She stopped when her breath hitched. Back then, the fear that he'd abandoned her was almost as bad as the thought of him lying dead in a gutter somewhere. "But I couldn't find you. It wasn't until I got here that I learned that you had given me a fake last name. Why would you do that? Why lie to me?"

He took her hands and pulled her over to the couch. This time, however, he didn't drag her onto his lap but he kept hold of her hands as they sat. "Growing up with my name…was hard. The Girard name has been both a blessing and a curse. The money opened no end of doors, but I felt as if I was being coddled because of my father—because of my name." Alex caught her eyes with a glance. "I wanted to go to school abroad where no one knew who I was. I'd wanted that for as long as I could remember."

"But why not tell me once we'd gotten serious?"

He shook his head sadly. "I don't know. I would guess that I planned to. I was probably about to. Once I knew that you loved me for me and not for my wealth or connections." Alex lifted his head to look at her questioningly.

"I did." She'd loved him more than she thought she was capable of loving anyone.

"But not anymore."

Maia wasn't sure how to respond to that. She was falling for him again, of that she was sure. But they were both very different people now. Who knew if they would able to make things work? Should they even try? Perhaps this was better off as closure to a bad phase of her life. Something that she should enjoy for now then just move on. She had become so bad at gauging relationships that she couldn't say what was going on between them.

"That's so unfair. We've only just become reacquainted. And until now, you didn't even truly believe I was telling you the truth." And that hurt. She'd hated him for a very long time. But knowing that hate was based on a misconception... It changed everything. But even a place like this and fantastic sex with the one man who she'd ever truly loved wouldn't erase the pain that quickly. In her mind, they might as well be starting from square one.

He regarded her silently.

Because she already knew the answer was no, Maia asked, "Do you love me?" Alex clenched his jaw, but no reply was forthcoming. Just as she'd expected.

"Then you can't expect me to be able to say that I love you, can you?"

Point proven, she sat back a little. The fantasy vacation was truly over.

Alex wasn't happy to let her shift away and took her hand in his, keeping her from moving too far out of reach. "I know that I'm not ready for this to end."

She wasn't either. But were they deluding themselves? "Maybe we should take things a little slower."

He frowned but he nodded, taking his hand back. "If that's what you wish."

Maia noted the way his face blanked and the light in his eyes faded a little. "You've just had a huge bombshell dropped on you."

His eyes narrowed. "Don't pin this on me. I know what I can handle. If you want to turn tail and run, just say so."

Irked by his words as much as the truth behind them, she sighed. "I'm not running. I just need a little space."

"Very well." He stood and regarded her grimly.

She followed him and got to her feet but stepped in his path when he tried to walk past her. "Alex. We both need a minute. You can't be fine after hearing all that and discussing it brings back some bad memories. It was a very dark time for me. You understand that, don't you?"

He glowered at her. "Of course I do. I'm not a monster."

"Then could you please just take a moment and breathe?"

"There are so many unanswered questions." He took her hands and stared her straight in the eyes. "I dislike not knowing. I hate that I wasn't there for you. I hate myself for not being able to remember. You are the only one who can answer most of my questions."

Maia couldn't say no to that. She just wished there was a way to show him everything without having to be the one to tell him. "Then ask."

"How can I when you shut down at the slightest provocation?"

"All I said was that I needed a minute. Besides..." Maia tightened her grip on his hands. "Everything is out in the open now. So if you have something to say, to ask, just do it."

Alex scrubbed his hand over his face. "I don't want to do it like this. Come."

Maia stayed rooted to the spot. "Come where?"

He tugged on their linked hands. "Will you just humor me?"

She hesitated only a fraction of a second before allowing him to lead her to the boxes. He silently pulled out the candles and the prepared meals. The food was quickly laid out on the coffee table, then he lit the candles one by one.

"Please sit." He pulled out a bottle of wine and deftly uncorked it, pouring her glass first, then his own. "That's better."

Was it? She sat and lifted the lid to the meal. It was simple, a crisp salad and chilled chicken, but it was their proposed topic of conversation that left her cold. Still, with the lit candles, it looked wonderful.

Alex sat and picked up his glass. He sat silently watching her a moment before taking a long drink. "I don't want to bring back bad memories. The last thing I want to do is hurt you more. But could you please tell me how we met?"

Maia remembered it well. The memory brought a small smile to her lips. "I actually tripped and fell into you. I burned you with my coffee."

"So you throwing drinks at me has been ongoing since the beginning." Alex chuckled.

Heat crept into her cheeks. "Well, that time, it was an accident. I was nervous about the first week at the university. It was the first time I was away from my home and family."

He smiled sympathetically. "So how did I react?"

"You were really nice, actually. Even offered to buy me another coffee." That had turned into their first coffee date of many. "I agreed only when you let me pay for your dry cleaning. That cost a bit more than I was expecting. I had to skip lunch for a week."

Alex shook his head. "I wouldn't have let you do that had I'd known."

Maia knew that. He wasn't one to let people suffer if he could help. "It was a point of pride for me. I ruined your shirt. I was going to fix it."

They ate silently for a little while. Maia figured Alex was slowly assimilating the information, spreading out his questions so she wouldn't get too upset. She wasn't sure if it was better to slowly let the feelings back in with the memories or to tell him everything in one fell swoop and deal with the fallout afterward. But she complied. It was great to finally let everything out.

Talking it out with him allowed her to remember all the good times they'd had. The fun that their younger selves could afford that seemed silly now. It put a smile on her face recalling just how young and in love they had been. Up until his disappearance, what they'd had was good.

* * * *

By the time they finished the last of the wine, Maia had told him about their first year together. Alex listened intently, asking questions every now and then. But for the most part he sat silently and absorbed everything she told him, processing it.

Maia followed his lead when he started clearing up the plates. They stayed silent up until he started wiping the tabletop, and she couldn't take it any longer.

Maia delicately tugged the cloth from his hands and dropped it to the table then took his hands and tugged on them until he looked at her. "What are you thinking?"

He looked at her with sad eyes and sighed heavily. "That if it wasn't for my accident we would have really had a chance at happily ever after."

Maia's stomach churned with his words. She didn't want to think about what ifs. "Can you tell me what happened to you?"

"It's only fair." He led her over to the couch. But instead of sitting, he got down on his knees in front of her. He smirked wryly when she hesitated a little. "I want you to feel this." Taking her hand, he pressed it to the back of his head to follow a jagged scar that ran up nearly to his right temple.

She traced the horrific reminder of his accident that had been hidden beneath his hair. Maia had no idea it had been that bad. "Oh, my God." Tears welled up in her eyes as she let her fingers travel up and down the raised line.

"So you understand just how terrible the accident was." He kept hold of her hand when he sat next to her. "You remember I returned home because my mother was ill." He continued when she nodded. "She passed away not too long after I arrived."

Maia clutched his hand. "I'm so sorry."

His lips tilted in a small smile of thanks. "I have no recollection of the accident or much leading up to it. Father tells me that the night it happened I'd taken off full of sadness and rage and with nowhere to channel it. I hadn't had anything to drink. I was just blinded by anger and helplessness. From the police reports, it seemed I tried to take a corner too fast. And since the corner was on the side of a cliff…"

Her breath hitched. It was a miracle he was alive.

"If I had taken just a little care… If I hadn't been such an idiot… Things would have turned out very differently."

She let go of his hands to cup his cheeks and turn his face toward her. "It's not your fault."

"It feels like it."

"Can't we just leave it up to fate? It might have torn us apart, but we've managed to find each other again. What matters is what we do with the time we have now."

Alex's gaze flickered down to her lips before catching her eyes again. "Something I intend to make the most of."

And he kissed her.

Chapter Thirteen

Alex plundered her mouth her with a desperation that made her heart ache. She hated that he took all the responsibility on himself. Even if she did the same at one time, knowing what she did now, what he had been through, she could never blame him for any of it.

Maia tangled her fingers in his hair, sliding over the ridge of the scar. She traced the raised length of it, the horror of what he had been through bringing tears to her eyes. She met his biting kisses fiercely, glad that they had this moment together. As unlikely as it was, they'd managed to find each other again. Perhaps it was time she started believing in fate once more.

She pulled away from him and smirked at the questioning glance he gave her. She had no plans on stopping him. His expression turned to dawning appreciation when she slipped the straps off her shoulders and let the dress glide down her body to pool at her feet. Seeing as she hadn't been able to find any underwear that suited the occasion, she was bare beneath.

Biting back a moan, he returned his hands to her skin, caressing everything within reach as he made his way down her body. His head dipped as he took the aching tip of one breast between his lips, flicking at the hardened bud with his tongue on his way down.

He slid his hands down her sides and hooked around her hips. Alex used his knees to slide her feet apart so he could settle his mouth between her thighs.

Maia's head fell back as he opened his mouth against her. She wavered under his erotic onslaught. Her hands returned to his hair out of passion as much as to keep upright.

Alex skillfully used a combination of his mouth, tongue and fingers to bring her to a shattering climax that left her reeling and breathless.

When she finally came back to herself, she found herself sprawled across his lap on the floor. The storm still raged outside the building, but she felt calm. Languid. And it was no wonder. The man under her had completely shattered her senses. And from the insistent movement of his hands and hips, he wasn't about to let up.

With a quick shift, she straddled his hips as he quickly shucked his jeans and donned a condom. Then he was arching into her in one long thrust. He gripped her hips and started rocking a pace that had her working to keep up and beating him to a spectacular orgasm just moments before he joined her.

She fell against him, replete and exhilarated at the same time. Alex smiled up at her, but it didn't quite reach his eyes. It came across as resigned. Tired.

Maia wasn't going to let him slip back into a funk. "Come on. The floor's cold." But instead of leading him down to the bedroom, she pulled him over to the couch. "We can watch the storm."

* * * *

And that was what they did for the next two days. They talked and watched the storm ebb and rage, as they indulged in each other as often as they could. With everything out in the open, Maia felt as if they were starting with a clean slate. But she couldn't figure out what was going through Alex's head.

When they were intimate, it was as if she was the only thing in the world to him. But afterward she would catch him in moments with a lost, almost haunted look on his face. When she asked what was bothering him, he would simply snap out of it and kiss her until she couldn't think straight. She would let him get away with it for now, but she would hash it out with him before they returned to the real world.

A look out of the window now reminded her that they didn't have much time left in seclusion. Soon they would be back in their lives and who knew how that would change things.

She watched morosely as the slowing rain dripped off the edge of the roof. The wind was calming. The ocean was returning to its former crystalline blue and the sky was no longer an ominous gray. Everything was going back to the way it should be.

Why was that such an unsettling idea?

"Maia?"

She turned to find Alex holding the satellite phone. "Hey."

He noticed her mood. She could see it in his eyes. There was a pause as he studied her. Alex held up the phone. "I just got word that the weather has cleared enough for us to leave."

It seemed that he wasn't as reluctant to return to their lives as she was. Her heart felt as though it was filling with lead as she nodded. "I'll get packed."

"Maia?"

"I'm fine. I'll just get my things."

"Hey, now." He deftly stepped into her path and swept her into his arms. "Nothing needs to change when we get back."

She had to smile a little at his optimism. "Of course it does. We both have to return to our lives once we leave this place. I've already done my articles for your hotels. Once I've sent them off, I have to get to the next destination."

Alex's eyebrows dropped thoughtfully as he ignored her attempt at changing the subject. "We *will* make things work. I can visit you and vice versa."

"Yeah." It came out even less enthusiastically than she felt and Alex picked up on it if his frown was anything to go by. Thankfully, he let it drop. At least for the moment.

* * * *

The flight back was quiet. Maia took the easy way out and pretended to edit and write on her laptop while Alex seemed quite happy to let her bury her head in the sand as he made a series of calls ranging from arrangements for a ride from the airport to various calls that she wasn't proficient enough in French to translate.

She chalked them up to business. To ask would prove that she wasn't as intent on her work as she made out to be. She did hear the name Angelique mentioned a few times, though, as well as her own. And not knowing why their names were being uttered made her stomach clench.

By the time they made it through the airport and were being loaded into a limo, Maia's stomach was in knots and her mood had soured considerably.

"You've been quiet," said Alex as he settled into the plush interior next to her. "Everything okay?"

She'd sent off her articles to her editor and already got a gushing reception for them. Her next assignment had been arranged and all she had to do now was gather her things from the hotel and she'd be ready to take off again. Everything was exactly as it should be. Everything was in order, but she felt as if her life was inside out. "I got everything sent off and I got my next assignment."

He frowned. "Already? Where are you headed next?"

"Mexico. There's a new resort opening up on the Riviera Maya. I leave pretty much as soon as I can get packed and back to the airport."

Alex kept his eyes on her as he pressed a button and said two sharp words to the driver. The car almost immediately swerved to the curb and stopped.

"Alex? What are you doing?"

His presence filled the small space. "You can't go yet. We need to figure this out."

She pressed her fingers to her temples. "We've been over this. We can figure out whatever this is as we go."

Alex gritted his teeth. "And cram in a relationship where and when it fits? What you're doing is running."

She straightened her spine and stared right back at him. "I'm trying to be an adult. We're not kids anymore and we can't just expect things to fall together just because we want them to."

"And nothing happens for people who just wait for it to fall into place." He ran his fingers over her cheek.

She sighed. "You said yourself that we can visit each other. Why don't you come with me? You could call it a research trip."

Alex frowned, shaking his head. "You know I can't right now. I have to oversee the development of another property."

Maia crossed her arms and sat back to stare at him. "But it's okay to ask me to hit pause on my life so that it'll fit in with yours?"

He scowled at her, but it softened as he pulled her close. "Of course not. I just thought we would have more time together before you flitted off again."

Maia wound her arms around his neck. "I guess I don't have to rush off right away. I'm sure I could spare a few hours if there was something worth my time."

"Only a few hours?" Alex punched the ceiling a couple of times and the car started moving again.

She shrugged. "I guess I could adjust my schedule accordingly. Depending on what comes up."

Smirking, he twisted her under him, making very sure he proved that there was something definitely up. "We have at least thirty minutes before we get to the hotel."

"Oh?" Maia wriggled under him. "I guess we'd better make the most of it."

He didn't need any more encouragement. Impatient, Alex pushed her top up so he could caress her breasts through the thin silk barrier of her bra. He nipped the delicate skin under her ear. "I can't get enough of you, Maia."

She knew the feeling. Being with Alex was like a wonderful addiction. The more she had of him, the more she wanted. And right now, Maia needed him. Needed to know she wasn't the only one who felt this way.

After undoing his belt and the button of his trousers, she edged the zipper down so she could slip her hand under his clothes. He thrust into her hand when she closed it around as much as she could of his erection, bringing a smile to her lips. Maia reveled in the power she had over him. That she could have Alex trembling from a touch awed her. It inspired her to see how else he would react if she continued.

Not to be outdone, Alex quickly got past the barrier of her clothing to stroke her clit with delicate brushes of his fingers.

Maia tightened her grip on him and slid her hand up and down his cock, amping up the tension in his body with each stroke. Just like he was doing to her with his clever fingers.

Her breath came in gasps and sighs when he plunged his fingers into her, grazing the little bundle of nerves with his palm as he pumped his hand.

Just as she convulsed and exploded under him, he crushed her mouth under his as he took her cries into himself.

Dazed, Maia stared up at him, fighting to catch her breath.

Alex grinned down at her, kissing her again before slowly slipping his hand out from between them. "We should almost be at the hotel."

Reluctantly, she released him.

Alex sat back and righted his clothes while Maia did the same. And not a moment too soon. Within seconds of her running her fingers through her hair and tying it in a neat knot at the back of her head, the limo came to a stop.

They all but ran through the lobby and up to Alex's suite, leaving their luggage downstairs, not really caring what happened to it.

All that mattered was getting upstairs and in his arms again.

He shoved the door open then dragged her inside to push her against the door and attack her clothes with single-minded determination.

Within seconds, he had her hair down and her clothes off and flung aside so he could see, touch and taste her skin. Everywhere.

He pressed her hands over her head with one hand as he explored her with the other in tandem with his lips and tongue.

Alex licked and kissed her on the mouth, her throat, her breasts. He dropped to his knees and hitched one of hers to his shoulder to press a hot, open-mouthed kiss between her thighs.

Maia let her head drop back against the door with a dull thud as the pleasure streaked through her. After only a few days together, Alex learned very quickly what he needed to do to have her quaking under his ministrations.

It took him minutes to bring her to orgasm using his mouth alone.

Trembling from the aftershocks, she could only hang on when he swept her up in his arms and carried her to his bed.

Placed gently among the pillows, Maia watched as he undressed. He was beautiful. Strong and well built—he was perfect. With each bit of clothing he lost, she grew surer of the fact until he stood before her, proudly naked.

Maia couldn't help but stare at him. He was too handsome not to.

Alex let her look her fill for a moment longer before he slid up her body to settle himself against her.

Arching into him, she sighed at the sensation of the head of his erection sliding over her.

Tension thrummed through Alex. Just as she thought he was going to plunge into her, he stopped and rolled to his back. He smiled wolfishly at her as crooked his finger in a beckoning gesture. Maia didn't hesitate and slid over him, straddling his hard thighs.

Alex took himself in hand, rubbing the head of his cock over her slit, lubricating himself before pulling her down over him and sinking deep into Maia.

Gripping her ass, he helped her up and down his erection. Slowly dragging her over him, thrusting up when he drew her down.

Maia held on. There was nothing else she could do thanks to the incredible sensations Alex sparked in her. Jaw slack from the pleasure, she cried out his name in time with his thrusts until she convulsed around him again.

He tightened his arms around her, pounding into her, building her up to another even more powerful orgasm as he drove toward his own.

Maia tipped back toward the bed and he followed without missing a thrust. She could feel him getting bigger, harder, with every thrust until he groaned as he pulsed inside her.

They lay entwined as they recovered, staring into each other's eyes. Alex kissed her as if he needed her more than his next breath. It wasn't about exciting her, or him. It was gentle, languid. Loving. They were two people connecting. Two compatible souls that had found each other and were entangled, not willing to let the intimacy end.

A long while later, Alex eased out of her and wound himself around her as if he would never let go.

Maia didn't want him to.

Needless to say, she didn't make it onto a plane until late afternoon the next day.

Chapter Fourteen

Maia dropped her bag on the floor and stepped into her small flat. It wasn't much, but it was hers and it was the perfect place to hide out until she got her head sorted out and had to travel to her next assignment. She felt a little guilty at misleading Alex. She did have her next assignment all arranged, it just wasn't as immediate as she'd made it out to be.

But the feelings coursing through her were beginning to frighten her a little. Not to mention the night before they'd had sex without a condom. The fact that it hadn't even occurred to either of them to use one at the time was a definite factor in her needing space. Maia figured there wasn't much risk, considering where she was in her cycle, but it had still left her shaken enough to run.

Alex hadn't even seemed to have realized, if he had, there was little chance she would have been able to get away as easily.

A niggling little voice whispered at the back of her mind. Could it have been all a ploy on his part?

Maia couldn't believe that he would be so callous.

But the idea of having his baby caused heat to bloom in her heart. A stubborn little girl, just like her daddy...

She shook off the image of an adorable, chubby baby with his dark hair and eyes.

How could she be so stupid?

Drained and jet-lagged, Maia didn't have the mental capacity to deal with just how colossal an idiot she had been at the moment.

She checked the email from Jo and sighed. A few edits, which was expected and details about the next destination. She would make the changes and send them off before she was on her way to the airport again.

Maia quickly opened the windows. She punched the couch a few times and watched as the dust puffed from the fabric. There was no way she could stand this. When was the last time she'd been here? She couldn't even remember.

It took her a few hours, but Maia eradicated every bit of dust from all corners of the flat. The physical activity helped clear her head a little and reminded her why she had moved there in the first place. It was cozy and just enough to live in for the short visits she made to it.

But it was boring. She barely had any furniture. There was very little in the form of mementoes. She didn't have any art anywhere, nothing that she picked up on her trips was on display. And why should she when she was never there to enjoy them? Maia looked at the bare walls and shook her head. It was no wonder she never wanted to be here, it was barely a home.

With a sigh, she pulled out her laptop and wandered into the kitchen with it to read over edits while she made a cup of coffee. A look at the time reminded her that she hadn't had anything to eat since she'd left Nice. And that was only because Alex had practically fed her the meal. She didn't exactly feel like eating anything still, but flipped through her stack of takeout menus to see if anything struck her fancy.

Nothing did.

She found a pack of dried noodles and refused to look at the use by date because she knew it would be either very close to being over or well out of date by now. A quick mental debate had her throwing it out. Coffee would be fine.

Her phone pinged and she couldn't help but smirk when Alex's name flashed on her screen.

Miss you.

And she missed him too. More than she should when they were only together several hours before.

She quickly texted back.

Miss you too.

She felt guilt close its claws on her gut.

The coffee wasn't the best she'd ever had, but it was good enough to stop her stomach from rolling. What was she doing? She'd lied to him when he'd been nothing but honest and straightforward with her.

He hadn't mentioned anything to her about Angelique, though. She should have just sucked it up and asked him why he was talking about her on the flight back from Belize. Doubt started to plague the back of her mind. Would he go back to her?

She slumped over and pressed her head against the cool countertop. He wasn't the type to juggle women. But then how much would she actually know about him after only spending a short time with him?

He was probably wondering the same thing about her, come to think of it.

Maia had to remind herself that for her their relationship had started years ago while for him they had only just met.

It was a truly mind-boggling situation. It hurt her head to process it all.

Instead, she lost herself in her work.

* * * *

Alex smiled at her text and fired one in reply before getting back to work. Not that he was able to concentrate. He caught himself staring into space more than a few times since he'd arrived on the site.

And again, when a hand on his shoulder drew him back to reality.

His father regarded him with an indulgent smile. "You look smitten."

Alex chuckled. "I'll try to hide it better."

Guillaume shook his head, joining his son in laughter. "Don't. It looks good on you."

"And how will I assert my authority when I'm staring into space like a besotted fool?"

"I see your point." Guillaume continued to smile. "I take it you and Maia sorted things out."

"I'm not sure we've discussed everything." There was still so much that he didn't know about her. He wanted to learn everything and wished he'd had more time to do it before she left.

The knowing smile on his father's face didn't budge. "I'm glad you two found each other again. It seems to have done you some good. I hope she's doing better as well."

Alex wasn't so sure about that. She had seemed distracted before she'd left. Distant. But she was probably thinking about her next assignment. Although, she had been quiet since they left the island.

"Have you spoken to Angelique since you've returned?"

Alex nodded. "I have. I've made it clear that things have ended."

"And you're going to continue with Maia?" his father hedged.

That was the plan. Alex turned to his father then. "Why so interested, Papa?"

Guillaume shrugged. "I just want you to be happy. And I haven't seen you like this in a very long time."

"And you think Maia will make me happy?" He already knew the answer. After their trip, he felt lighter. The weight of his responsibilities no longer dragged him down. He found that he enjoyed spending time with her and missed her when she wasn't around. Sharing ideas with her had become routine over the past couple of weeks. Alex was amazed at how they had both opened up so much over such a short time span. Then again, they weren't exactly the most conventional couple.

"Hasn't she already?" His father clapped him over the shoulder again. "But I sense that not everything is good."

"I want to remember what happened between us before. Maia's told me about our relationship and…everything. But I want to remember. I've looked at everything that Marcel brought out of storage a million times over, but nothing. It's like a gaping hole in my head. I see the photos of us and it's like catching a glimpse of another reality. I want to be able to recall what made us laugh in them. What made her smile."

"I see. Have you told Maia this?"

"She says that it doesn't matter. That we should be happy with what we have now."

His father nodded sagely. "I agree with her. If she's told you everything and it's in the past, why should it matter?"

"Because it matters to me." He knew he sounded like an obstinate child, but it was how he felt. He wanted to remember everything about her. It killed him that they'd been through so much together and he could recall none of it.

"But why does it matter so much? You should think about that. What if in your search for the past you forget the present?"

Alex sighed. "I want to talk to the doctor who treated me after the accident again. And the best neurologist I can find."

"Son." His father's tone held a note of warning to it.

"Papa." Alex refused to back down. He wanted to go down every avenue before admitting defeat.

"Just take a step back and really look at what you are doing. Is it purely selfish? If you are truly going to commit yourself to Maia, then you should consider her and her needs as well." With that he sauntered away.

Of course it was for Maia as well. She deserved to have someone who could remember her. Who could remember everything that she could.

He pulled out his phone and did a quick search for the best neurologist in the field.

Chapter Fifteen

A week later, Maia motioned for the porter to take the rest of her things into the room.

As promised, the hotel was part of a luxurious resort that was simply stunning to look at. It filled her vision as it sprawled white on the white sand, contrasting starkly with the darkening sky and water.

It was perfect in the setting.

She just hoped that everything else would be as well.

Maia took mental notes as she followed the porter through the lobby and to her room. As the porter stepped in with her things, she caught a glimpse of the stunning interior. It was more like an apartment than a hotel suite. She loved the huge windows and the fresh flowers had to be her favorite feature, though the lush furnishings were a close second. And that was only what she could see from the door.

She couldn't wait to explore it further.

It may have been perfection, but she felt less than enthused to be there. Alone, at least. She missed Alex. The texts they sent back and forth almost constantly didn't cheer her up at all and the few video chats they'd had were plagued by lag, bad connections and time constraints. It just reinforced the idea that they were drifting apart.

But before she could start dwelling, a familiar voice forced her back to the present.

"Hello, neighbor."

Sighing, Maia turned next door. Would it be petty to dock points from the hotel for the porter being too slow to get her stuff in and get out? She knew she was cranky and tired from the flight and chastised herself mentally before smiling tightly at her coworker. "What are you doing here, Chloe?"

"Jo thought we made a great team last time and sent me here to do my thing." Her scornful gaze raked over Maia. "What the hell happened to you? You look terrible."

She felt it. "Thanks so much."

Chloe smirked. "Did you two fight the entire time you were on that island?"

"It's none of your business."

"There were bets going around, you know. You two were either going to kill or tear each other's clothes off. I guess the former was what happened. I owe people some cash."

If she only knew the truth. Maia just rolled her eyes. "Is this why you're talking to me? To confirm a bet?"

Her coworker's smirk grew. "Partly. Another is to point out that a mutual friend is here as well." She pulled out her phone before she looked pointedly down the hall.

Even though she didn't want to, Maia followed her line of sight to find Tomas unlocking a door. He chose that moment to look up and smiled warmly. "Maia,

Chloe, what a surprise." He waved the porter in and walked over to them to give Maia a hug and a peck on the cheek before doing the same to Chloe. "Are you two on another assignment?"

"Yeah. It's quite a coincidence seeing you here," Chloe purred, grinning in a way that reminded Maia of a piranha. Did the woman ever stop?

"Quite a coincidence." He smiled at Maia, leaning in close to whisper. "I'm just checking out the competition." He stepped back a little. "Is Alex around? I had something I wanted to talk to him about, but he hasn't responded to my calls or emails."

She shook her head. "He's busy with another project at the moment. I'm sure he'll get back to you as soon as he can."

"You sound like his secretary." Laughing, Chloe linked her arm through Tomas'. "How about we go see what this place has to offer?"

Tomas nodded, even as he slipped his arm out of her grip. "What do you say, Maia?"

It was on the tip of her tongue to refuse. She wasn't in the mood to hang out, but Maia knew she had to do something to get herself out of her funk. And irritating Chloe might just do that. "Sure. Just give me a second."

Maia grabbed her purse, swapped her shoes and took a quick look at herself in the mirror. Hair in a ponytail, rumpled jeans, wrinkled white shirt and sandals that were almost worn through. Not exactly glamorous but it would do.

"Ready. So what did you want to do first?"

"I could do with a meal." Tomas looked at the pouting Chloe before settling his gaze on Maia.

"Sounds good." Not really, but it gave them something to do. At the very least, it might give her something to write about.

They settled for a beautiful onsite restaurant, one of several apparently, and chatted over drinks as they waited. Chloe sat across from Maia while Tomas took the seat next to Maia. She was dimly aware of Chloe snapping pictures on her phone, which wasn't all that unusual. She should probably be doing the same thing. Maia couldn't find the energy to pull her phone out.

Tomas' voice drew her attention. "So what have you been up to, Maia?"

"She and Alex were stuck on an island together for a week," Chloe interjected, so helpfully.

He nodded approvingly. "Sounds ideal."

"It was lovely." Maia's tight tone didn't even sound convincing to herself.

"So lovely he's chosen to work instead of spending more time with you." Chloe didn't even try for subtlety.

"We both realize we have commitments." Why was she even justifying herself to the other woman? She'd already spent enough time pondering and wallowing. Maia had come out with them to enjoy herself and this was far from what she wanted. "You know what? I'm a bit tired. I think I'm just going to try to get some sleep."

She got up and left before either could say anything.

Maia didn't get very far before she heard heavy footsteps behind her.

"What was that about?" Tomas closed his hand over her shoulder, slowing her down.

She didn't have the strength to shrug him off. "Chloe's just being her usual charming self."

He didn't look as though he cared too much about the reasons, just in her. "Are you okay?"

"I'm fine. I don't usually let her get to me. I'm just too tired to deal with her bull today."

"She does seem to enjoy antagonizing you." Tomas fell into step next to her. "Don't let her get to you. She's only looking to get a reaction."

"I know. Like I said, usually I can handle it." Maia sighed. All she wanted right now was a long, hot bath, preferably with Alex, then to get in bed. Again, preferably with Alex.

Tomas smiled encouragingly. "Feel like a walk on the beach? It always relaxes me."

"Yeah, I remember." She started to shake her head, but reconsidered. What was she going to do in her room alone? Mope? She'd spend hours tossing and turning and she knew it. "You know what? I could use some exercise after such a long flight."

His smile was brilliant. "Wonderful."

Silently, they headed for the sound of the ocean. The moment they hit the sand, Maia slowed to take off her sandals. The sensation of warm sand on her feet relaxed her.

"Good idea." Tomas did the same, rolling up his trouser legs at the same time.

Their leisurely stroll buoyed her mood. It felt nice to just wander aimlessly and work out the kinks.

"You're quiet. A lot on your mind?" Tomas asked softly.

"Yes and no."

He chuckled. "If you want to talk about Alex, that's fine, you know. I wasn't lying when I said I was happy for you two."

Did she really want to talk to Tomas about another man? "What makes you think what's going on in my head has anything to do with Alex?"

"Just a look you have." Tomas hesitated, keeping his piercing blues eyes on hers. "Are you sure everything is all right between you two? You seem sad."

Still so sweet. She forced a smile, even if it was the last thing she felt like doing. Maia crossed her heart. "Jet lag. I swear."

"Good." He shoved his hands in his pockets and kept walking.

Awkwardness started to settle in. She cleared her throat. "How have you been?"

He scoffed. "Good. Work keeps me busy."

"I'm glad you've been good." Much better than this conversation was going, she hoped. Maia sighed. "The truth is, I don't really know how it's going between me and Alex. It's complicated."

"Oh?"

The slight press of his hand on her arm stopped her. Maia looked at him for a split second before turning to stare at the water.

"Remember the man I told you about. The one who had hurt me?"

Even in the darkness, she could see his expression turned grim. "Yes."

"It turns out he didn't know what he had done. He'd had an accident and that's why he never came back. He lost his memories."

Tomas took in the information with a nod. "So it *was* Alex."

Maia was mildly surprised he had guessed who she was talking about but not really. "I guess you know about his accident, huh?"

"Alex and I have been friends for a while." He frowned. "I had wondered why you two were so awkward with each other at the party. I thought it might be because of my presence." He sighed. "So I had misunderstood how close you were then, but now…?"

Maia was thankful that the night hid the blush heating her cheeks. "Things have gotten a bit more complicated since then."

"I gathered that." He let out a slow breath. "I can tell you that Alex isn't one to play around. He's not that kind of guy."

"So Angelique… He's been with her a while?"

An understanding smile spread over his lips. "Not as long as you think, I'm sure. And as far as I know, from gossip in our circles, he's moved on to a beautiful writer."

"Really?" Her heart felt like it was going to burst.

Tomas smiled. "Yes. And from the smile on your face, I'm guessing I resolved your dilemma."

A part of it. On a whim, she hugged him. "Thanks, Tomas."

"No problem." He hugged her back before taking a step away. "Shall we continue our walk?"

"I would love that."

Hearing what she had from Tomas made her steps lighter. Her heart too. They wandered down the long beach. Maia ambled with her head back for part of the walk to stare at the sea of stars above.

"If you keep that up, you're going to end up in the ocean."

"I'm sure you'll make sure that doesn't happen." Maia stopped to look at Tomas. "You are a wonderful man. I wish I could have been the one to make you happy."

He sighed and dragged her around to look at him. "It just wasn't meant to be. And you did for a time. I'll never forget that."

"I'm still sorry about what I did."

His smile was small, but she believed him when he said, "I forgive you."

"Thank you."

They wandered a little while longer before heading into the hotel. They stopped in front of her door.

"Thanks again, Tomas. You've been a big help."

A smile curved his lips. "Of course." He pecked her on the cheek. "Goodnight."

"Goodnight, Tomas." She patted him on the shoulder.

As she entered her room, Maia dialed Alex, but for some reason he wasn't answering. So she sent him a text bidding him a good night. It wasn't until she got out of the shower that she received a curt *Goodnight* in return. He usually wanted to catch up for a bit.

Maia chalked it up to fatigue on both their parts. She'd text him again in the morning when all her brain cells were working once more.

* * * *

Alex put the phone down, irritated that the text had derailed his train of thought. He'd been doing mountains of research on memory loss, neurological trauma and all things associated with both. It seemed there was a wealth of information on the topics but not enough to satisfy him.

His calls to experts hadn't yielded much more. They all seemed to agree that if the memories hadn't come back by now, they weren't likely to.

Alex scrolled through the text on the webpage. It was all beginning to blur together in a morass of hopelessness. Still, he wasn't ready to give up. He wanted his memories. All of them. Everything about their time together.

Up until he found the truth about his past, it didn't really matter to him that he'd forgotten a large chunk of his life. How much could he have experienced in that time? It was a rationalization that he'd made many times. What could he have forgotten but boring classes and monotonous university life?

What indeed. Could he have been more wrong?

Alex glared at a photo of their younger selves smiling blissfully into the camera and was torn between tearing it up and tracing her up-curved lips with his finger. He settled on the latter.

He'd lost his first meeting with Maia, getting to know her, the first time they'd made love. It was frustrating to know that he couldn't remember her favorite drink, or food. That he'd lost their entire relationship devastated and infuriated him at the same time. And he'd just let it go without a fight? That rankled worst of all.

He'd barely recovered from the accident before he'd simply moved on with his life. Finished with his schooling in Paris, he'd dived straight into work for the Girard Group. It never even occurred to him that he'd left anyone behind. And he'd let her down in the worst way possible.

He wasn't going to just lie down and take it. He would rectify his sins against her.

Alex picked up the phone again to call the number on the webpage. He would see if this one was worthy of calling himself the best neurologist in the world.

Chapter Sixteen

Three weeks later, Maia stood looking down a rough Incan pathway, wondering how best to capture the image. With her phone or with her camera? She opted for both, sending the image she captured on her phone to Instagram when she was happy with it. She flipped through the past few uploads she'd made and smiled ruefully when she came to the ones of her and Alex's trip to the ruins in Belize.

She hadn't heard from him in weeks and before that, his texts had grown sparse and buffered by silences that were growing lengthier each time. Maia rationalized it for as long as she could, but even she had to admit that he was losing, or had already lost, interest.

What did she expect?

They were both too busy to maintain a lasting relationship. And, well, didn't most men have a wandering eye? What made her think that Alex would be any different?

Because Tomas told her he wasn't? Because she wanted him to be? Because she thought he was the love of her life? She had let girlish hopes of happily ever after cloud her judgment. Maia couldn't believe just how stupid she had been to get caught up in all that again.

A solitary tear ran down her cheek and she angrily swiped it away. No tears. Not this time.

If he could just walk away from her, why couldn't she do the same? Gritting her teeth, she sighed. She hated that he had done this to her. That he could affect her so deeply. She should have learned her lesson the first time.

Thinking about him soured her mood, so she forced him out of her mind to focus on the sheer beauty of where she was. Of what she was looking at. That lasted about forty seconds.

Her phone pinged, reminding her that she was there to work, not just gawk. When she looked at her screen, she didn't expect to see Tomas' name there.

Mildly surprised, she swiped her thumb across the screen.

M, I think you should see these. I was only just alerted to them. It looks like your coworker is out to start some trouble. T

She scrolled down to see pictures showing her and Tomas when they were at that resort at the same time. There were several photos, but the ones of her kissing him on the cheek and of them having drinks together grabbed her attention. The photos managed to make them look like a couple enjoying intimate moments in each other's company. She agreed with Tomas' assessment. They could have only been taken by one person—Chloe.

Maia quickly thanked Tomas via text and debated sending another to Alex in the hopes that he'd finally reply. His silence was message enough, really. Had he already seen the photos and taken them at face value? It was the only other explanation for his lack of response.

Did she truly want to try to continue a relationship with someone who would shut off from her without an explanation?

With a long, slow breath, she switched her phone back to camera and continued taking photos. She could push him out of her mind just as easily as he'd forgotten her. Maia wanted to. Desperately. Only she couldn't do it. How could she? If she gauged herself by the progress she'd made over the past few weeks, she'd have to say she was failing. Miserably. She kept wondering what he was up to. What he would do if he was here with her. What they would be doing together.

And it annoyed her. A lot.

But she got him out of her head once before and she could do it again.

Maia switched off the camera and dialed Jo. If anything would help clear her head, it would be a new location and a new adventure.

"Maia! The French Riviera special is a hit! I'm staring at an inordinately huge bouquet from Monsieur Girard thanking us. And they should! Your article on the Girard Group will be lining their pockets for years to come!" She laughed gleefully. "How're the ruins treating you?"

"It's gorgeous but dull. I need something with a little more adrenaline."

"And I thought you'd be worn out from Australia and Madagascar." A chuckle came from the other end.

"Right. There are quite a few of those coming up. What are you most interested in? We've got a jungle trek in Borneo, Singapore for the F1 Grand Prix, dogsledding in Iceland or a new luxury resort in Switzerland."

They all sounded fantastic. "How about all of the above?"

"That's ambitious." Jo paused a moment. "Is everything all right?"

"Of course. Can you blame me for wanting to get to all those before my competition?"

"Is this about Chloe?" Jo asked, her tone knowing.

Maia could see how Jo would jump to that conclusion. "No, but I do want to talk about those pictures for the last article. She took those without my permission."

Jo growled. "I see. I'll have a talk with her."

"Thanks."

There was a long pause. "Anything you want to talk about?"

They weren't the best of friends, but she and Maia had a good relationship. "Just in need of some diversion."

"Nothing to do with your being trapped on an island with a certain hotel mogul a few weeks ago?"

Maia sighed. "Chloe?"

"You seem to be on her mind a lot."

The woman was a nightmare. "I just need to clear my head."

"I get it. I've been there." Tapping on a keyboard came from Jo's end. "They're all yours if you're up for it. And remember, I'm always here if you need someone to talk to."

"Thanks." Maia smiled a little knowing her offer was genuine. "So what's up first?"

"Borneo for a week. From there it's just a hop to Singapore for a few days for the Grand Prix. From there it's Iceland then Switzerland."

"Sounds perfect." And hopefully she'd keep herself too busy to mope. "I'll talk to you soon."

She hung up and reverted back to the camera.

Maia couldn't wait, especially for a trip to Iceland and the Alps. The ice and snow were just what she needed to snap her out of her melancholy. She could already imagine days filled with skiing and nights writing by the fire, watching the snow drift by the window.

The thought alone made her smile a little.

Solitude was what she needed. It didn't hurt that the solitude she craved and was going to get was accompanied by five-star accommodations.

Maia sighed and she followed her guide. It had been so easy to fall back into Alex's arms. It was understandable. Logical. There had been so much that went unsaid that seeing him again was bound to bring everything back to the surface.

She had let herself have her little fantasy. Even had a little revenge. She smirked as she remembered throwing the champagne. It felt like a lifetime ago. She'd found out the truth, said her peace, and they'd enjoyed each other's company and that was enough.

It had to be.

So she had lost her head a little with Alex. She would have judged herself if she hadn't. He was her first love and he'd grown into a spectacular man. Devilishly handsome, smart, driven. Maia would have thought herself irretrievably damaged if her head hadn't been turned by that.

And most of all, she'd finally gotten her closure.

She just had to wait for her heart to get the message.

* * * *

Fireworks burst high above, adding to the jovial mood of the night, but Maia just couldn't get into the spirit. The opening night of the Singapore F1 Grand Prix should have been fun, exciting even, but she watched it all from behind her camera. She might as well have been watching it all through a webcam.

At least she got some amazing photos for her article.

Neither the energy from the crowds nor the music from the concert penetrated the haze of misery that cloaked her. As much as she tried, no matter how exotic or exciting the locale, Maia couldn't stop thinking about Alex and how much he'd hurt her yet again.

She blamed herself for letting him in. Him for being an ass. Even her job got the blame for a little while for bringing him back into her life.

Maia quickly checked her phone for notifications, even though she knew it was pointless. Her calls, texts and messages hadn't been returned. It was obvious he had cut her from his life and she needed to get it through her thick skull.

He didn't want her.

Gritting her teeth, she took more pictures, preferring to focus on the beautiful scenery than what seemed like an endless stream of happy couples.

Making her way through the throng of glamorous people, she looked for a new vantage point for more photos and maybe a new angle for her article. So far all she had to write about was how stunning everything was.

"How did you enjoy the festivities?"

Maia turned to find a handsome man with dark hair, a wolfish smile and beautifully tailored suit smiling at her. She noticed the way other women eyed him, but she couldn't say she was as taken by him as they were. "It was great. Just like the concert and the venue."

He smiled and lifted two champagne flutes from a passing tray. "For having witnessed something so great, you don't seem so enthused."

Maia refused the drink when he offered it and didn't reply, hoping he would take the hint and go away.

He wasn't deterred. "Are you at least excited about the race tomorrow?"

She shrugged and edged away. Why wouldn't he take the hint? There were plenty of women vying for his attention and he wanted the one woman who didn't want it.

"Have you ever seen an F1 race? If you had, you would know how exhilarating it is."

She smiled wanly. "I'm actually here on business."

"As am I. I'm going to win the race." He boasted loudly enough to draw more eyes toward them.

Maia's first instinct was to leave, but getting an account of the race from a driver's perspective would be more interesting than just 'it was amazing to watch'. "I'm sure the other drivers would say the same."

Apparently glad that he had finally got some response out of her, he grinned. "But the others would be wrong." He held out his hand. "Riccardo Vitalli."

She took it and tried not to grimace when he kissed her knuckles. "Maia Reynolds."

"A pleasure." He purred. "Why don't you join me and some friends? We're having a party to celebrate." He pointed to a group of suitably glamorous people watching them avidly.

A party on top of a party. Wonderful. "I can't stay long, sadly." His smile was cajoling, but it left her cold. "I told you I'm here on business."

"And what kind of business is that?" He stepped closer.

Maia edged back. "I'm a travel writer here to cover the race."

It was apparent that he relished the thought of getting more publicity. "Then you will want to talk to the best driver here."

"I would like that." She eyed him up and down. "But I want you to know that I'm only after the story. Nothing more."

He put his hands up as he chuckled. "Of course."

He led them to a table overlooking the water. Above, fireworks exploded, cascading the night sky with shimmering sparks and cameras flashed all around as the music hit a crescendo. It was something Alex would enjoy. At least she thought he might.

Maia ruthlessly shoved the thought of Alex aside. What he liked or didn't like was of no matter to her. She hated that she couldn't get him completely out of her mind. What bothered her more was when thoughts of him snuck up on her without warning. It always left a hollow feeling in her chest and tears threatening to fall.

"Maia? Are you okay?"

Not really. "I'm fine." She forced a cheerful smile and set up her phone to record their conversation. "So, Riccardo, tell me about yourself."

* * * *

Alex stared up at the sterile white walls. How many identical walls had he been faced with over the last few weeks? And for what? It was pointless.

With a growl, he sat up and tore the sensors from his scalp.

"Monsieur Girard!" The disembodied voice came from a hidden speaker seconds before a small army of lab coats flooded into the room.

He slid off the table and glared at them all. "This isn't working."

"We can't give up, monsieur." The head researcher held the sensors out pleadingly. "We've only just begun."

Alex glared at him. He couldn't even remember his name after all the doctors in white lab coats he'd been through in the past few weeks.

He'd heard that more than a few times now. And each occasion had been a failure. "You've done enough tests."

"But..."

So far nothing had worked. It seemed the diagnosis of the doctor who had originally treated him had been right. There was not much of a chance he was getting his memory back. At least none that they could find at the moment.

"If you can think of a new tactic, call me." Alex had had his fill of hospital, clinics and labs. Especially since no one seemed to have a clue about what they were doing.

No one stopped him as he slipped on his jacket and walked out.

He navigated the choked Parisian traffic and drove back to his apartment in Paris' eighth *arrondissement*. The building had been built in 1900 but had been refurbished luxuriously earlier in the year before being put on the market. He'd bought it the moment he'd laid eyes on it, having been drawn to the light and space and clean lines.

He opened the window to let in the breeze and took a moment to look at the iconic Eiffel Tower etched into the sky in the distance. The view wasn't too bad either.

Alex walked into the spacious living room and straight into the stacks of boxes. The contents of each had been carefully sorted. The things he considered important had been removed and were now gracing his desk and any other surface with a spare bit of space.

A stuffed bear smiled at him from his chair while framed photos of Maia's younger self beamed back at him with equal happiness as he sat.

He smiled back at her, but it quickly melted away. As much as he stared at the photos and mementoes, nothing came back to him. It was as though he was looking at someone else's belongings. Someone else's life.

He hated that no matter how hard he tried, how hard he worked at it, no memories were sparked. For the first time he was being beaten. Alex wasn't going to take it lying down. He would regain his memories.

He retrieved his tablet and scrolled through the list of names and deleted the last.

On to the next.

Chapter Seventeen

Maia stepped out of the airport and took a deep breath. After the long flight, wandering through the airport in Zurich felt fantastic. Unlike the other passengers who rushed to get through customs and out of the airport, Maia took a more leisurely approach. She wasn't in any hurry. Taking a moment to just stretch her cramped limbs, she pulled out her phone and texted Jo to let her know that she had landed and that she would be off the planned path for a while.

Since she was a few days early, she fully intended on doing a little sightseeing and shopping before heading up to the resort in Zermatt.

She got the cab to take the scenic route through the city, something the driver had absolutely no problem with. On his way to drop her off at the hotel she'd booked only days before, he announced interesting locations and pointed out things that most tourists missed. She'd heard it mentioned before as being the perfect hotel in the perfect location for sightseeing in the city. So far, from what she saw so far, it was just that. Perfection.

Maia got out and looked up at the soaring building. The gleaming glass construct sat in the heart of the city straddling the line between the commercial and financial districts and no doubt made the most of both when it came to travelers for business and tourism.

With that in mind, she walked in and smiled. Where some hotels smacked patrons in the face with attempts to prove their lavishness, what she experienced in the lobby was a restrained luxury that took a discerning eye to fully appreciate. The gleaming marble floors and furniture, which she recognized as the work of a famous artisan, all whispered extravagance.

She loved it.

That was until she got to her room and flopped on the bed. On her way down into the heavenly soft down comforter, she caught a glimpse of the hotel logo on the corner of a pristine white sheet. There was no mistaking the interlocking golden G insignia.

Maia shot off the bed as if it was on fire. She grabbed the brochure off the desk and scanned it. Maia almost snorted when she got to the part where they gleefully announced they had recently joined the illustrious Girard Group.

Some travel writer she was. Why hadn't she taken a closer look before booking?

She was exhausted, preoccupied and running from the memory of Alex, that's why.

There was no way she was going to stay the night. Cursing her inattention, Maia smacked herself in the head with the brochure before putting it back in place. As she kicked her things toward the door, realization hit her and she shook her head. She was acting like a child. A cowardly and petulant one at that.

Taking a few deep breaths, she collected herself. She refused to scamper like a frightened little girl. Maia straightened her shoulders. She would leave, but not before she'd had something to eat. It would be a shame not to sample what the Girards had on offer. She might even be able to link this experience to the article on their hotel in Nice.

Locking the door behind her, she made her way down to the restaurant as her critical eye kicked in. Not that there was much to critique. Like everything else she'd seen of their hotels, it was superb.

Maia barely studied the menu before ordering. Despite the fatigue and the fact that she'd eaten on the plane, she was more than ready for a three course meal. At least.

While she waited, she sat back and took in the ambience. She could almost imagine the other patrons being hired actors to complete the scene. Everything screamed opulence and luxury. There wasn't a thing that didn't fit or was an inch out of place.

She let her mind wander as she listened to the conversations around her. It was something Maia enjoyed doing. Traveling alone, it became almost a game to try to guess who the speaker was, where they were from. Just listening to the voices and their accents, it didn't even matter that she couldn't understand most of what was being said. She liked the rhythms and cadence, imagining what they might be saying.

It made it easier for her to home in on conversations in English, however. As the two gentlemen behind her had drawn her attention with their Australian accents.

She half listened as they discussed business, but then her ears perked when they mentioned their upcoming trip to Zermatt.

"But we'd best leave soon," said the one closest to her. "I hear there's a storm coming and it's going to be a big one."

"No worries. I'll just get the bookings changed and we'll leave straight away."

Just what Maia was thinking. She pulled out her phone and started dialing.

At least this way she didn't have to admit to herself that she was running from another reminder of Alex.

Chapter Eighteen

Alex swore and threw his tablet across the room. He watched with grim satisfaction as it shattered and fell to the floor in pieces.

"Bad news?"

And, of course, his father had to be there to witness his slip of composure. "Just some disappointing news, Papa."

"Just disappointing?" He eyed the remnants of the tablet skeptically. "What happens when you get news that's truly upsetting?"

He huffed an amused breath. "You don't want to know."

That made his father smile a little. "Was that the latest doctor, then?"

Alex didn't really want to share the news with his father but knew that he wouldn't leave without discussing things. "No one thinks that they can do anything to help me."

"Thinks or knows they can do nothing?"

"I know what you're going to say." As much as he hated to admit it, it was probably time to admit that there was nothing that was going to bring his memory back.

"Don't you think that it's time to give up on it, then?"

Alex was thinking the same thing. How long had he wasted on this madness? He'd flown back from Paris a few nights before and had checked in with the specialists in Nice for a report that hadn't met his expectations.

"Have you spoken to Maia lately?"

He hadn't. He'd been so caught up in research and traveling between experts and work sites he barely had time to sleep let alone text or call Maia. Alex was sure they could survive time apart. Wasn't she the one who insisted they be grown-ups?

"No. Why do you ask?"

His father pulled out a copy of *Pulse*. Alex had read Maia's report on their hotels and was pleased with the result. The spread was tasteful and detailed with photos that were alluring.

Alex nodded approvingly before his father produced another issue of the magazine. He chuckled. "Checking out the competition, Papa?"

Guillaume ignored his son's comment. He quickly flipped through to find the page that he wanted, folded the magazine back and handed it to his son.

Alex took it and read. It was an article by Chloe about the nightlife at the new resort in Mexico that Maia had been sent to. The other woman's writing wasn't at the same level as Maia's. It was quick, to the point. Hardly compelling. He scanned her drivel about the amazing restaurants. That was until his eyes reached the photos. His jaw clenched the instant he saw the pictures. Maia and Tomas. It was as if something in his head imploded with each photo. They looked so content. Sharing a smile over their meal, walking together on the resort grounds, there was even a picture of Maia pulling him closer.

Jealousy, pain, anger all hit his gut at once. He didn't want to believe that she would cheat on him but photos didn't lie. How could she betray him? It was true he hadn't called her or texted in a little while but did that warrant her running off with someone else?

His father handed him another one with a feature on the Singapore F1 where Maia was at a table with racer and notorious womanizer Riccardo Vitalli, enjoying drinks. He crushed the magazines in his hand and tossed them aside. "Thank you for bringing this to my attention, Papa."

"I showed it to you because I wanted you to see what you were doing." He patted his son on the shoulder. "When was the last time you talked to Maia?"

"A few days ago." It wasn't the case and they both knew it. He revised his answer. "A couple of weeks."

"Are you sure?"

The tone of his father's voice irritated him, but he pulled out his phone to check his outgoing calls. According to the listed dates it had been a couple of months at least since he'd last called her. He had to have texted her more recently than that. He checked. Those too were far down the list. And there were a few texts from her that he hadn't seen. He flicked through them and he could see that she'd progressed from flirty, to worried, to resigned. The few messages she'd left were the same. He swore under his breath.

"It might not be as bad as you think. You know as well as I do how easily a photo can be manipulated and misconstrued."

Sure, it could have all been very innocent. But what were the odds of she and Tomas accidentally meeting up when he knew Maia was flitting from one side of the planet to the other while Tomas did the same? It had to take some coordination to find the time and meet.

Alex gritted his teeth. But from the way that she'd behaved when they were together, she was as enamored with him as he was with her. She had to be. He couldn't be the only one to feel the chemistry, the connection.

But she and Tomas did have a past. One that Tomas made clear he had been eager to resume. With him out of the way, had the other man simply stepped in? Had Maia let him?

Anger flared. Was this some game for her? A way to get back at him? She'd said she didn't blame him for how things ended the last time, but had she meant it? He had to wonder if her hatred of him ran deeper than even she realized.

Alex raked his hands through is hair. "When was that published?"

Guillaume shook his head. "The last is from this month. The other, from the month before."

"But the photos could have been taken at any time between this week and the last time I saw her, couldn't they?"

"It's fathomable. But I want you to use your head. I don't think that Maia would do anything to hurt you. If you look at the photos, it's all very innocent."

He didn't want to look at them again. But he picked up the magazines and smoothed the pages so he could get a better look. He scoured the images of Maia and Tomas closely. Sure enough they were just eating. Maia looked more interested in the content of her plate than what was going on around her. In the one of them walking, they weren't so much together as Tomas following her. And the one of her pulling him toward her, a closer inspection of her hand showed it was flat. She had been pushing him away. It didn't mean that it was all innocent off camera. His eyes zeroed in on the one of her kissing him on the cheek. But it didn't warrant jumping to conclusions either. Chloe had taken the pictures wanting things to look suggestive, even if there was nothing in them to warrant speculation.

Fury at himself and at Chloe descended in a red haze. He didn't even bother looking at the other magazine. He had been the one to push her away. If she thought he had cut her out of his life again, why wouldn't she look for someone else?

The thought of Maia in another man's arms twisted his gut.

Alex quickly picked up his phone and dialed. "If you'll excuse me, Papa, I've got some things to sort out."

"Of course, son." His father gave him a pat on the shoulder. "Just trust in your feelings for each another. Don't let outside forces influence you."

"Stop worrying, Papa." Alex couldn't say the same for himself. He studied his father a moment. He wasn't as concerned as Alex was. "You believe things will work out for us?"

"Son. You two are good together if only you could just get away from these walls you put up around yourselves. First you don't believe her, then she finally lets you in, then you find a way to distance yourself with this fool's errand." Guillaume closed his hands over Alex's shoulders. "You have a real chance at happiness here. Don't let it slip away because you can't let go of the past."

Guillaume left his son to contemplate what he was doing to his life.

* * * *

Maia got on the packed train to Zermatt not too long after dinner. Already the snow had started to come down. It was hard to imagine that the fluffy flakes would turn into something life-threatening as the world outside slept under a thick white blanket while they rushed past.

She settled back and attempted to do a little reading on her phone. It would be so easy right now just to curl up in a ball in her seat and fall asleep. Maia forced herself to focus on the words, refusing to give in to the urge.

The same page had been staring her in the face for quite some time when a pleasant voice over the PA broke the silence. The discontented murmurs from around her washed away the hazy clutches of sleep. Whatever was just said wasn't good news.

The voice spoke again, this time in English. "Please be advised that because of adverse weather conditions, we will be unable to continue to Zermatt..."

That was all Maia needed to hear. Skiing was going to have to wait, apparently.

It was chaos at the terminal. Inconvenienced travelers always made the worst kind of anarchy. She avoided all the shouting and finger pointing, searching instead for somewhere quiet to try to call and find out if there was any other way of getting to the resort.

Staring out at the snow, she dialed ahead to the resort but got nothing. Another call to Jo met the same fate. Cursing the god of cell reception, she looked around for an alternative. The few payphones were at the end of long, winding lines that discouraged her from joining.

She avoided them and headed toward the waiting area but that was filled as well. Maia was about to give up when she spotted the two Aussies from dinner. Looking for a little camaraderie, she headed over.

She was greeted with broad smiles. "G'day."

Maia gave them a small smile. "Not really. It looks like we're stuck here for a while."

They shared a look before they turned back to her. "Actually, we were able to get a helicopter to take us the rest of the way. If you want, we could give you a lift."

She looked at the curtain of white falling outside. "What about the weather?"

"It's not that bad yet. If we get out of here now, we can beat the worst of it." The tall one smiled. "Better than spending who knows how long stuck here, isn't it?"

It was. Almost anything with a bed would be at this point. "Which way?"

She received jovial claps on the back as they walked with her to the helipad.

* * * *

Maia kept a white-knuckled grip on the handle as the helicopter dipped and plunged as it was buffeted by the wind. Garrett and Dane, her two new friends from the Land Down Under, seemed to find her terror hilarious, like just about everything else. The two thrill seekers loved every moment of it.

"You have to meet up with us for some skiing. We can make a day of it. Or two!" Dane jostled her shoulder with his, chuckling when she flinched as the helicopter shuddered.

"If we survive this." They lurched again, throwing them up in the air for a second before crashing back into their seats.

That and her comment gained more uproarious laughter.

Maia ignored them in favor of concentrating her energy on not vomiting, passing out or falling out of the helicopter. The last two weren't likely, but the first…

"You guys have to let me pay for this." Her stomach rolled. Wasn't she paying for it already?

"Money is irrelevant. You come skiing with us and we'll call it even."

Maia wasn't sure if she agreed or not. All she wanted was to be on the ground again.

She closed her eyes and hung on.

Luckily the pilot felt the same way about getting to the ground ASAP and they flew to the car-free town in record time. The instant they landed, Garrett helped her out, while Dane took her bags. She must have looked really bad because their jovial mood was subdued as they helped her to the hotel.

She could only remember thanking them, the receptionist's concerned smile and a blurred trip to her room before falling face first into the bed.

First impressions of the place would have to wait until she could see straight.

* * * *

"I'm sorry, Mr. Girard. I can't tell you where Maia is."

Alex scrubbed his hand over his face. He'd finally managed to get a hold of Maia's editor, Jo, but the woman was being less than cooperative. "Please. I've been trying to get a hold of her and haven't been able to. Have you been able to reach her? Have you spoken to her lately? Gotten a text?"

There was a slight hesitation. "I heard from her a couple of days ago."

"But nothing since?" His stomach clenched. "I know she keeps in constant contact with you. The only time she didn't was when we were stuck in Belize. Are you telling me you aren't worried about her?"

"Are you saying you are?" she asked icily.

Had Maia been sharing with her boss about what was going on with them? "Of course I am. So if you could please tell me where she is—"

"I'm not going to do that, but when she checks in, I'll let her know you're looking for her."

He clenched his fist around the phone. It might not have been what he wanted but it was better than nothing.

Alex managed to grind out a less than pleasant sounding, "Thank you."

He hung up and dropped the phone on the table. Well, he'd gone and made a total mess of things. Maia was out there somewhere and he had no clue where. He couldn't find her. She wasn't answering his calls or his texts. He wasn't even sure if she was getting them or if she was ignoring him or had changed her number. Which he wouldn't blame her if she had done either one.

Alex could only imagine what she was thinking. What she thought of him. For the second time, he'd disappeared on her. Only this time he'd done exactly what she'd thought he'd done the first time. The irony was almost laughable.

He had to find her. All he wanted was a chance to explain. And perhaps beg for forgiveness.

That was if she would even give him the time of day. If he was Maia, he'd have a few choice words for him.

After his father had left him to think, Alex realized that what he was doing was insane. He had the chance for something new and pure and he had all but thrown it away because of his quest to sate his own desires. Not a thought was given to what Maia wanted or needed.

Maybe what she needs is someone else?

The thought of her with anyone other than himself veiled his vision in a red haze. It wasn't an option. He might not have been reunited with her for very long, but he knew that they belonged together. That he couldn't be without her.

An email notification pinged on his phone and Alex took a quick glance, sure that it would be nothing more than junk or status updates on work sites. But he caught Maia's name just before the screen went black again.

Snatching it from the table, he tapped the screen until the email opened in full. He had asked all the hotels within their scope to look out for her name and that of the magazine she worked for and even Chloe's name on the off chance that either of them had checked in. He never expected to see Maia's name since she seemed to be avoiding him, but there was always the chance. No matter how slim that was.

And as luck would have it, it had happened. The reservation was under her own name but according to the records, she'd checked out almost as soon as she'd checked in. It didn't matter. She had been in Zurich a few days ago. He did a quick search for any new resorts in the area and was rewarded with one in Zermatt. She had to be there.

Triumphant, he saved the information and immediately called his pilot. She was so close. He could be with her again within a few hours. He imagined her glowing and flushed as they made love next to a cozy fire and his body tightened in anticipation.

He outlined his intention to the pilot, but was surprised by the response.

"I'm afraid we can't travel to Zermatt right now, sir."

"Why not?" Alex was about ready to strangle the man through the phone. He needed to get to Maia and he wasn't going to take no for an answer.

There was an audible gulp from the man on the other end of the line. "The weather won't allow it. I can probably take you to Geneva but that might be as close as we'll be able to get."

Alex's stomach clenched. Maia was trapped in a storm? "Then Geneva it is. Be ready within the hour." If that was as close as he could get to her at the moment, he'd take it. There had to be other ways of getting to her and he'd find one once he got there. He would reach her even if the only way to get to her was by dogsled.

"Yes, sir."

Preparations for the trip were made quickly. Once he had told his father his intentions and made a quick stop in the city, Alex boarded the plane. He just hoped Maia was okay and that she would give him another chance.

Chapter Nineteen

Being cooped up inside the hotel wasn't as bad as it could have been. The hotel itself was a wonder and gave her plenty to see and do. It was nice not to have to rush from one place to the next for a change. The relaxed pace gave her time to explore the facilities and to write. To generally just unwind. Only, it was harder to do in practice than in theory.

The suite she had booked into was beautiful. Modern, lots of natural wood and panoramic views of the Matterhorn and the Zermatt Valley. Her favorite feature was the deep wooden bath that she'd already soaked in three times since she'd arrived. But even that hadn't helped ease the tension from her muscles.

Fatigue from all the traveling wore at her but sleep was plagued with dreams of Alex. When she woke, she was nauseated and feverish, making work a misery. Maia considered calling him, texting him. They had to talk things out. It was absurd that she'd let this go on as long as she had. She even tried dialing more than once but Mother Nature had won each time. Contacting him would just have to wait until the storm blew over.

In the meantime, she curled up with her phone to read on the chaise near the fire and willed herself to stop thinking about him.

After half an hour, Maia put the phone down and wrapped her arms around her head. The dull throbbing at her temple plaguing her the past few days had gotten worse. As had the nausea. She couldn't even look at the words on the screen any longer without them swimming and making her stomach roll even worse.

She hated to admit it but whatever this was, it wasn't going away on its own.

Maia stumbled over to the bed and dialed the front desk. Time to see if the medical services they offered were as amazing as the rest of the amenities.

Minutes later, there was a knock at the door. The small team that arrived was quick, polite, professional and gave her a diagnosis she half expected.

"I suspect you have a case of altitude sickness, Miss Reynolds. Unless you can think of another reason you feel this way?" The doctor smiled encouragingly. As if a smile was all he needed to get her to spill all her secrets.

Maia didn't have the strength to add anything. Every evening since she'd arrived at the hotel, Maia had stumbled into her room exhausted, head pounding and a tiny bit nauseated. She'd been at higher altitudes than this before and had been fine. More than fine. She blamed Garrett and Dane, the weather... The helicopter. They had obviously ascended too fast for her to handle. They'd beaten the storm, but at what cost? It probably didn't help that she hadn't been sleeping well in the past few weeks.

She had to do something about that. If she couldn't get herself back on track by the time she left Zermatt, she would have to get something to help. Maia nodded. "I'm sure that's what this is. Thank you, Doctor."

"You'll be fine in a few days. I suggest that you take it easy until then." He took a bemused glance at the snow-filled window. "Not that staying put now will be a problem, but you probably shouldn't go any higher once the weather clears. If it persists, please contact me immediately." He pointed at a small packet on the end table. "I've left some pamphlets for you to read as well as some tablets and other things you might want to take a look at."

"I will." At the moment, the only thing she wanted to do was get a little something to eat, have a hot bath and get in bed.

Once he'd gone, she snagged the room service menu off the nightstand and flipped through. Nothing looked appetizing. She dropped the little booklet back. Maia contemplated the bath but the bathroom was just too far away for her to bother. Rolling over, she buried her face in the cool pillows. She'd feel better in the morning.

Maia yanked her clothes off, leaving only her underwear to separate her from the cool sheets.

It felt heavenly.

* * * *

She must have dozed off, because the next thing she knew, there was a pounding at the door that reverberated through her skull, rattling her brain and making her moan from the resulting pain.

Maia burrowed deeper and pulled a thick pillow over her head, hoping to block the noise out.

"Maia!"

Her stomach flipped. *Alex?* Was she hallucinating?

She had to be. Pressing the heels of her hands to her temples, she burrowed back under the pillow only to have the knocking resume harder — louder.

Grumbling, Maia slid off the bed. Taking the sheets with her, she half shuffled, half stumbled to the door. The instant she unlocked it, it burst open and narrowly missed hitting her as it slammed into the wall.

Gripping the table next to the entrance, she watched Alex stalk into the room and scan it. He looked rumpled and tired.

And angry.

"What took you so long to answer?" he snarled.

"What?" He wasn't making any sense. Or was it her head that was muddling things up? Was he really there? Or was he a figment of her imagination? And if he was really there, what was he looking for?

"I asked you a question." Alex finally turned to look at her and his eyes widened. He caught her before she hit the ground and cradled her gently.

"*Dieu*, Maia! What's wrong?" He ran his hands over her, as if he was making sure she was whole.

She groaned when he jostled her. Gripping his arms to make him stop moving, she grunted. "Altitude sickness."

Alex muttered something under his breath that could only have been an expletive as he swept her up into his arms then gently placed her on the bed.

Maia ran her fingers down his cheek. "Are you really here?"

"I am and a good thing too." He carefully tucked her in and checked her temperature. "Have you been seen by a doctor yet?"

It took too much effort to nod. "Yeah."

Alex nodded and brushed a gentle kiss on her forehead. "Just get some rest. I'll take care of you."

When she heard that, Maia laughed ruefully as her vision dimmed. "Now I know I'm dreaming."

Alex didn't know what to expect when he knocked on her door. All he knew was that she was inside and that it was taking her too long to answer. All kinds of images flashed through his mind. Mostly of Maia naked with someone else and he lost it. If it had taken her a second longer to open the door, he couldn't say that he wouldn't have kicked it in.

But when he saw her looking so pale and obviously ill, everything but the urge to take care of her flew from his mind.

He sat on the edge of the bed watching over her. She looked frail, tired and definitely thinner than he remembered. Guilt gnawed at him. He'd done this to her. Didn't she say when he disappeared before she was so upset that she forgot to take care of herself? He just thanked his lucky stars that circumstances weren't exactly the same this time around. Though imagining her carrying his child made his heart throb a little.

Rubbing the section of chest over his heart with the heel of his hand, he kicked off his shoes and got undressed. He'd flown into Geneva and had to eventually bribe a vehicle out of a rental service to drive to Martigny. He would have driven the rest of the way to Täsch where he would have had to catch a train to go the rest of the way, but the storm had kept him cooling his heels worrying about her being stuck in the middle of it. The trip up to Zermatt had been the longest in his life. Alex couldn't remember the last time he'd slept or even had a decent meal. All that mattered had been getting to her.

He stripped down and slipped in beside Maia, wrapping himself around her. Now that they were together he had no intention of letting her go again.

Chapter Twenty

Maia tried to press her hand against her throbbing head, but it was trapped between her and a solid pillow. She leaned into it, enjoying that it was warm and felt like Alex.

And smelled like Alex…

Forcing her eyes to open, she found herself in his protective embrace, face against his chest. She let her head fall back so she could look at him. He was actually there! There were dark circles under his eyes and several days' worth of stubble roughened his jaw, but he had never looked better to her. What was he doing there?

He shifted making her aware that he was naked and very aroused. Maia tried to roll back but was trapped and she didn't have the strength to try any harder. Even that slight movement made her head throb painfully. Her attempt to muffle the groan wasn't successful.

Alex opened his eyes and loosened his grip a little, allowing her to move back but not letting go entirely. "Not feeling any better?"

"Not really." She took a moment to search his eyes. "What are you doing here?"

His eyes turned glacial. "Not glad to see me?"

That was the problem. She was *too* happy to see him. "Just wondering why you would suddenly show up when you've been ignoring me for weeks."

Alex sighed. "I'm sorry." He turned to his side to face her but the rocking of the bed had her dashing to the bathroom, despite her previous lack of energy.

Retching and hugging the toilet wasn't exactly how she expected to have that conversation. Maia collapsed against the tub when the heaving finally died down. With nothing to throw up, it had been a painfully fruitless exercise.

A hand swept her hair out of the way then caressed her back soothingly. "How long has this been going on?"

Maia's gaze was drawn to Alex's feet and traveled slowly upward. Thankfully, he'd put on his jeans but he hadn't bothered to do them up in his haste to get to her. Her survey of his body stumbled on the way they hung tantalizingly low on his hips. She would have looked farther up his body if she could, but tip her head back any more and she would be flat on her back.

As if divining that she didn't have the energy to lift her gaze any higher, he knelt down next to her and handed her a glass of water.

"It started when I got here."

Scowling he asked, "When was the last time you ate anything?"

It was humiliating that he was even there to see her sick, but to have him analyzing what he'd seen? She cringed. "I haven't been feeling too great the past few days. And I've been busy."

"So busy that you've run yourself into the ground."

"Back off, Alex." She glared at him as hard as she could manage. "Leave me alone."

"I won't. You need help."

"I'll be fine." To prove her point she pushed herself up and unsteadily made her way past him and back to the bed. "The hotel has a world-class medical team if I need it."

Alex stomped over to her and, despite her attempts to shove him off several times, eased her into bed and tucked the sheets around her. "You really are the most frustrating woman I've ever known."

He shucked the jeans and climbed in behind her.

Maia tried to shuffle away from contact with him but he hooked his arm around her, anchoring her to the spot. "What do you think you're doing?"

"I intend to take care of you. If that means pinning you to the bed, so be it."

Images of how he had pinned her to the bed in Belize made her breath catch a little. She tamped down the burgeoning desire. That wasn't going to happen.

"And you call me frustrating?"

Despite her words, Maia couldn't be bothered to struggle more. Not when it felt so good to be in his arms. She'd let him have his way for now. Just until she got better. Then she would send him packing.

Chapter Twenty-One

Alex luxuriated in the feel of Maia against him. He'd meant it when he said he'd pin her to the bed if he had to. Only he hoped that she would get well soon so that he could do it in a way that would be much more mutually satisfying. The thought of making love to her had his body hardening in response.

With a sigh, he dropped his head to nuzzle her neck. It was obvious that she was angry. Even as ill as she was he could see it. Feel it. Of course she was. He didn't blame her. Convincing her to forgive him would be a pain, or it could be exquisite torture. Alex hoped it would be the latter. As a plan, kissing her into submission had its merits.

In the meantime, he would take care of her as he hadn't done the last time.

Dawn hadn't brought much sunlight, thankfully. Maia still slept soundly and he wanted her to get as much rest as she needed. He stayed wrapped around her as long as he could, knowing she wouldn't let him once she was awake.

Alex took a look over the suite from where he was. Not bad. He'd have to wait to give it a more critical once-over but what he saw was pleasing to his discriminating eye.

A quick glance at the window let him know that the snow was slowing, but still hadn't stopped. He didn't care. Now that he was with Maia, he couldn't care less what was happening outside. She was safe.

Experimentally, he shifted. Bolstered when the rhythm of her breathing didn't change, he reached for the phone and called room service. Since he knew she hadn't eaten, he ordered one of nearly everything the restaurant offered for breakfast and pre-ordered for lunch and dinner as well.

Alex hung up, but as he brought his arm back to the warmth of the blankets, he accidentally brushed a small stack of papers and boxes. Medical advice from the look of them. Easing his arm out from under her, he rolled onto his back to read through them all. It wouldn't hurt to learn more about what she was going through in order to help her out more effectively.

He quickly read the information and sorted through the boxes of medication. Maia hadn't seen fit to use any of them if their pristine condition was anything to go by. He picked up the final unopened box and nearly dropped it when he saw what it was.

A pregnancy test.

He gripped it in his fist as he looked at her. Had Maia requested a test? Did she suspect she was carrying his child? Hope buoyed his heart. If she was pregnant, she would need him. She would stay with him. Wouldn't she? There was no way he could let her go if there was a baby.

But how could there be a baby? They'd used a condom every time, hadn't they? Alex pressed his fingers to his temple against the angry throbbing that came with the nagging voice in the back of his mind that it might not be his.

He recounted every moment they had spent together. Thankfully, his new memories with Maia were in high definition and he could remember every second of it.

Alex had trouble breathing when he realized that the night before she left they hadn't used a condom.

Shoving everything else aside he eased himself around her again, gingerly pressing his palm against her stomach as if he could discern by touch if there was new life nestled there. He couldn't help the smirk as the image of a boy with her dark hair flitted into his mind. Or would it be a little girl with his eyes and her smile? It didn't matter. He would love either and he would make sure any child of his had a father.

Alex pressed a kiss to her shoulder, sliding his hand up from her abdomen to cup her breasts through the lace of her bra. A happy sigh escaped her lips and she wriggled closer. Taking that as a good sign, Alex nipped at her neck, forging ahead cautiously. The last thing he needed was to push her too far. Pregnant or not, she was in a delicate state. He wasn't going to be the one to compromise her health.

Tipping her toward him, he kissed a path down over her collarbone to close over the hard tip of her breast.

Maia arched under him when his tongue flicked over her nipple. The shock waves that rocketed through her body brought a gasp to her lips. The sound, sadly, made Alex stop to look at her with a strange grin.

"Feeling better?" Alex looked hopeful.

She was, mostly. Maia refused to admit that sleeping in his arms was exactly what she'd needed. She hadn't slept as well since they were last together. Her head still swam a little and her stomach rolled. Breakfast would hopefully set her to rights.

As much as she was loath to, Maia put some space between them. "I could use a little breakfast."

His eyes darkened somewhat, but Alex nodded and backed away. "Of course. I ordered us some. It should be here soon."

She shoved aside the disappointment at him giving up so easily, then she slid to the other side of the bed. "I'll just get showered."

"Do you need any help?" Before she could reply, he'd put on the jeans he'd discarded the night before and rounded the bed.

Maia stood gingerly, keeping a hold of the bed until she was sure she was steady. "I think a bath might be better."

"I'll get it ready for you." Alex helped her sit before heading to the bathroom.

Not sure what to make of his knight in shining armor act, Maia sat back. Her memory was hazy, but she knew there had been a storm. She looked at the window. And it was still going on from the look of it. Had he braved a storm to get to her? Why? He had been the one to ignore her. Then the look on his face when he barged into the room. The way he'd searched. He expected her to be here with someone else?

Anger started to gnaw at her gut. "Alex?"

"Yes?" He sauntered out of the bathroom, followed by a plume of steam.

Maia kept her eyes on his face, not daring to let her gaze stray lower. She protected herself with a tightly wrapped sheet. "Why are you here?"

"We'll discuss that in a little while. First you'll have your bath." He draped an arm around her waist and walked her to the bathroom. "Need help getting in?" His attention slid downward, reminding her of her lack of clothing beneath the bedclothes.

She shook her head. The last thing she needed was his hands on her bare skin. Maia wanted to figure him out and needed all her brain cells in working order to do it.

His smile was crooked and utterly charming when there was a light knock at the door. "I'll get that."

Maia was neck deep in bubbles when Alex strode in. Jerking into a sitting position, it took her a second to attribute his appreciative smirk to the slow slide of bubbles down her chest. Slumping back down, she glared at him.

Totally unfazed, he balanced the tray on the curve at one end of the bath and made a show of unbuttoning his jeans. They fell to pool at his feet then he kicked them negligently aside.

Maia spluttered unintelligibly at the sight of him proudly naked before her. "What do you think you're doing?" She couldn't make herself look away. Her gaze traversed his sculpted form with unabashed delight.

Completely unperturbed by her scrutiny, Alex eased himself into the opposite end and took up the tray again, holding it on his knees. "I didn't want to delay your meal. You look half starved. So I thought I would join you." When she started to argue, he shoved a plump strawberry between her lips. "Eat first. You can better yell at me on a full stomach."

There was logic in that. Her stomach rumbled in agreement. She accepted his offering and chewed. "Fine."

He tore off a bit of crêpe and fed it to her before popping what she'd left into his mouth. The way he regarded her made her stomach flip. It was like he hadn't seen her in years. By all accounts, he appeared thrilled to be there with her.

She scowled.

"What?" He pilfered a dollop of whipped cream off a stack of waffles and offered it to her. When she shook her head, he licked it off with a long swipe of his tongue.

Maia's mouth went dry. "Why are you looking at me like that?"

"Like what?" He innocently chewed another bite of crêpe.

She picked up a slice of melon and took a nibble. "Like I'm a shiny new toy that you just got for Christmas."

"I'm just happy that you haven't kicked me out." He caught her gaze.

"It's still early." She ate the melon and reached for the waffles. Alex pulled them out of reach and tore the corner off one and fed it to her.

Maia studied him as she chewed. "What were you searching for when you first arrived?"

A sheepish expression spread over his face. "Honestly, I don't know. You took so long answering the door that I was afraid..."

Alex afraid? She didn't know he was capable of fear. "Of?"

Taking a deep breath he sighed. "That you wouldn't open the door. That you had found someone else. That you were here with him and I no longer had a chance with you. That you were no longer interested in me."

Maia frowned, her mind tripping over her tangled thoughts. "That makes no sense. You were the one to start ignoring me."

The sheepish expression on Alex's face twisted into a pained one. "I'm so sorry. I swear that I didn't mean to. I just got a little obsessed."

"With what? Those photos of me and Tomas?"

Alex reached down and placed the tray on the floor. "No. And we have to talk about your coworker Chloe and this vendetta she seems to have against you." He waved the mention of the other woman away. "Later."

"All right." It was a relief that he had enough faith in her that he wasn't angry about the photos. Maia was confused. "So then why did you ignore my texts and calls?"

Alex took her hands. The tub was big enough for him to be able to spin Maia around and settle her between his legs. He closed his arms around her, caging her against his chest.

Pressing his lips against her neck, he whispered, "I'm so sorry."

Her skin tingled wherever they touched. Molten heat followed the paths his fingers took as they traced patterns on her skin. Maia let her head fall back onto his shoulder to gaze up into his eyes.

The dark blue pools were deep, fathomless. "I lost sight of what was really important. I became so obsessed with recovering my memories that I gave up making new ones with you."

That wasn't what she was expecting.

Stunned, she leaned forward and twisted around to face him. She knew how persistent he could be when he wanted answers. Alex would move mountains to get what he wanted. Just how far did he go to regain his memories?

Fear chilled her, pricking goosebumps on her skin. "What did you do?"

He put his hands on her arms, sliding them in gentle, calming circles. "Nothing as terrible as you're imagining. I sought experts, subjected myself to testing and experiments." Alex sighed and hugged her tighter. "I wasted too much time on a pointless pursuit. I gained nothing and lost time with you in the process." He kissed her gently. "I hope you can forgive me."

She stared at him, incredulous. Relieved. "Of course I can. I thought…"

Alex chuckled ruefully. "That I had abandoned you again? That I found someone else that was better for me than you?" He slanted his mouth over hers, kissing her breath away. "Never."

Her head was reeling from all the new information. Her heart full, nearly bursting. "When those photos of me and Tomas were printed and you had stopped answering me altogether, I thought you had tired of me."

"Impossible. I could never tire of you." He reached down to pluck more food from the plate and held it out for her to eat. "Now, I'm going to make sure you've eaten and are healthy. Then I'm going to make love to you until the storm blows over."

Chapter Twenty-Two

"Do you think this will be an ongoing thing with us?"

Alex shifted so he could look into her eyes. They had settled in front of the fire near the window so they could watch the snow. Maia felt right snuggled against his chest. After their heart to heart in the bath, the atmosphere had shifted. They became two lovers trapped together in yet another maelstrom. Not that he was complaining.

He held her closer. "You mean the storm? I wouldn't mind if it was. As long as I'm with you, I couldn't care less where I am or what's going on around us."

She laughed. "I like it too. It's like there's no one else but us."

Alex nuzzled the delicate skin below her ear, inhaling her sweet scent. "As far as I'm concerned, there isn't."

"Maybe I should change my angle to storm chaser, then? I'm sure I could convince Jo to go along with it."

He grinned at her teasing tone. Wherever she went, he would follow, but he sure as hell wouldn't let her run headfirst into a storm. "How are you feeling?"

Maia wasn't as pale or wan as when he first saw her. She still wasn't as steady as he'd like, but definitely improved.

"Much better. Still a little wobbly but overall, I'm good."

"I'm glad. Because I need to ask you something." Alex eased out from behind her and sat in front of her. Straddling the chaise, he took her hands. "Is it possible that your illness might not entirely be due to the altitude?"

It took a second for her to catch on. Her eyes widened and her lips pursed adorably as she considered his question. "I don't know. It's certainly possible..."

"I only ask because I saw the pregnancy test on the bedside table. I wasn't sure if you had asked for it or if it was left just in case. I guess that answers that."

Maia's cheeks flushed. "I wasn't exactly in a talkative mood when the doctor was here. I remember him saying he left stuff for me to look at. I guess he was thinking along the same lines as you are." She paused. Her eyebrows dropped as she caught his gaze. "Is that why you're being so nice?" Maia tried to pull her hands away from his.

Something that felt too close to panic flared in his chest. He had to stop that line of thought before things got out of hand. "Of course not!"

"Alex. If you're just trying to make up for the past..." Maia's eyes watered. "You don't have to. If you're only here because you think I'm pregnant—"

His hands tightened on hers. "Maia. If you are carrying my child, then I will be over the moon. If not, then we'll just have to try harder. But I'm here for you. I want only you." He kissed her. "Just you."

What was it about Alex that sent her emotions out of control? One second she was happy, then angry, tense and now just plain confused.

Was he truly there for her or was he only being so nice because he wanted to make up for the past? Because he didn't want to abandon her, possibly pregnant, again? It hurt her head, and her heart, to think about it.

She stared at him for a long moment trying to divine his true intentions. There was one way of getting rid of one of the doubts.

Maia got up and stomped over to grab the stack of boxes from the end table and headed for the bathroom.

"Maia?"

She closed the door behind her. It was a simple matter to sift through the pile until she found what she wanted.

If she was pregnant, what would it mean? Before she had been a terrified student but Alex had assured her that he was going to be by her side. And that hadn't worked out. The situation was a bit different now. Maia had her own place, her own money, so those weren't a problem, but she had a career to think about and without that the first two wouldn't last. How long could she keep up the traveling with a baby to think about?

Alex seemed sincere. She wanted to believe that he was there for her and that if there was going to be a baby that he would love him or her as much as she would.

Maia took the test, replaced the cap and stared at it. It was funny how a little plastic stick could determine the fate of so many things at once.

The thing was, she didn't want her life to be dictated by it or anything else. She had let her emotions run her life for far too long. Now it was time to use her head.

Alex was wonderful, smart, sexy and he cared for her. He was perfect. He was even willing to scramble his mind to get his memories of their time together back. They clicked so well in and out of bed. Maia couldn't ask for a better partner.

She put the test face down on the counter, took a deep breath and, with her heart pounding in her ears, walked back into the bedroom.

Alex stood at the window, hands in his pockets, tense and pensively staring at the snow. He turned to her the moment she opened the door, an expectant expression on his face. "Well?"

"It's going to take a minute." She took a breath. Held it. Released it and did it again.

He crossed the room and wound his arms around her. "I meant it when I said I want only you."

Maia shimmied back a little, needing to see his eyes. "I know."

Alex shook his head. "I don't think you do." He tugged her over to the chaise and sat her at the foot of it. "I thought that I needed my memories to complete our relationship. But I know now that what we have is already complete. We have each other. We can make new memories."

She watched in a daze as he lowered himself down on one knee. He pulled a small box out of the pocket of his jeans. It was opened to reveal a dazzling diamond surrounded by tiny ones all set in glossy platinum. Maia's heart lurched into her throat.

"That's why I bought this for you before I left Nice. I know that I want to be with you. I need to be with you.

Maia, I love you." He took her nerveless hand and slid the ring on. "Please, marry me."

She launched herself into his arms. He'd bought her a ring before he'd left. He didn't know where she was or anything about a damned pregnancy test and he'd still wanted to marry her.

"I love you too, Alex. So much." Dragging his head down, she grinned before her lips met his for a scorching kiss. She drew back after a long while, both to refill her lungs and to say, "I've been so lost without you. You were right about me running myself into the ground. Without you, my life is hollow. It's just travel without the fun or the enjoyment. I need you in my life. You make me whole."

Alex grinned and didn't hesitate to dive back in for another searing kiss. Tongue dueling with hers, he groaned when her hand grazed his erection. "Are you sure you're up for this?"

Maia tore at his jeans. "What do you think?" It had been far too long. With his jeans out of the way, she ripped his shirt open, sending buttons flying into the far reaches of the room.

"I'm glad I'm not the only eager one." Chuckling, he made short work of her clothes tugging them off her with swift and decisive moves. Once she was bare, he let his hands and eyes trail over her skin. Alex picked her up and hooked her legs around his hips as he carried her to the bed.

He laid her on it as if she was made of spun glass. Alex grinned down at her. "I've missed you so much." He grazed his hands up her legs with feather-light strokes.

Maia loved the care he was taking with her but she needed him now. She didn't want soft and gentle. She wanted him wild and unbidden, ready and willing to push her over the edge again and again. But when she tried to drag him over her, he resisted.

"Patience."

"I've been patient enough." Hooking a leg around his, she pushed him over and straddled his hips. Maia changed her angle so she could feel him wedged against her and wriggled her hips. "Are you saying that you'd rather take it slow instead of taking me right here, right now?"

She let her hair trail over his chest as she slowly slid down over him. Maia rocked gently. "We could take it slow, I guess. Soft and quiet. But wouldn't you rather make me scream your name?"

She could see the instant his control snapped. Gripping her hips, he drove upward. Alex sat up, sliding his hands up her back to claw in her hair. "You know there's nothing I would deny you." He nibbled her bottom lip as he bucked into her.

Maia skyrocketed toward bliss. Arching against him, meeting his urgency with her own. With a biting kiss, he flipped her under him and drove even deeper. The words he growled against her breasts were a tangle of English and French. But she understood that she was loved. Cherished. His.

She climaxed with a keening cry. His name on her lips as she had promised.

Alex, wild and uninhibited exactly as she wanted him, drove her over the edge twice more before he finally joined her with a deep groan.

As they lay intertwined and gasping, basking in the afterglow, he ran his hands over her skin and sighed. "I could do this forever."

Maia laughed. "Could you imagine what Jo and your father would say to the idea of their favorite workhorses lying around naked all day?"

He kept hold of her as he rolled to his back, sprawling her over him. "I can't speak for Jo, but I think that my father would be delighted that we've finally decided to marry."

"We have? I don't remember agreeing to that." With a squeal, she evaded his halfhearted attempt to grab her. Maia slipped off the bed and dashed into the bathroom with a grin.

He watched her disappear into the bathroom and stretched, feeling languid and relaxed for the first time in weeks. The smile on his face wouldn't be budged.

Alex chuckled. He didn't have any doubt what her answer would be, but he asked, "So? What's your answer?"

"Yes." She stuck her head out of the door with a grin and waved the test. "And yes."

Epilogue

"Félicitations! Nous vous souhaitons à tous les deux tout le bonheur du monde!"

Cheers went up from around the room as Maia and Alex walked into their wedding reception.

They had returned to Nice a week before after spending another blissful week in Zermatt ensconced in their little haven. They'd spent the days enjoying each other and making plans for the future. It had been a struggle to leave. Maia couldn't imagine anything more romantic.

It wasn't until they'd arrived in Nice that she realized that he had taken the details of what would make her dream wedding that he'd ferreted from her while they were snowed in and made it happen. The week leading up to that morning had been filled with cake tastings and gown fittings and flowers until every detail was perfect. What made it even better was that Alex had been with her every step of the way.

They'd also taken a trip to the obstetrician almost the moment they landed to confirm that the test was accurate. And it was, but, for the moment, it was their little secret.

Alex pulled out her seat for her as they took their places at the head table. Maia looked out at the crowd of people. Smiling friends and family filled the tables. Guillaume sat proudly at the table nearest to them. Jo and Tomas were two faces that she spotted among the others through the pale rose centerpieces. Her editor winked while Tomas smiled and nodded his approval. She grinned back with all the happiness she felt.

Alex waved over a waitress just as the toasts started. She brought over two glasses filled with what looked like champagne. He leaned in. "Ginger ale for us both for a few months, no?"

With a giggle she took up her glass. With each toast, she and Alex took sips smiling conspiratorially over their glasses at each other.

They were enjoying the meal when Guillaume came over. "You two look so happy." He kissed Maia on one cheek then the other. "I couldn't be more pleased to welcome you to our family, my dear."

She hugged him. "Thank you." Maia caught Alex's gaze. He did look very happy as he gazed at her. The scowl that was almost always on his face when she first arrived in Nice was gone. The deep furrow on his brow had smoothed out. Alex looked at peace. And very much in love.

Guillaume whispered something to his son, who choked back a laugh, before he smiled at Maia once again. "I expect a dance or two with you later, my dear." He pecked her on the cheeks again and disappeared into the sea of guests.

"What was that about?"

With a shrug he chuckled, "I'll tell you later. We've got more people coming to speak with us."

Jo sashayed her way to their table and pulled a chair from nearby to sit next to Maia. "Congrats, you two!" The hug she gave Maia was sloppy. It was clear that she had a few drinks in her. "I just wanted to tell you that I've taken action against Chloe. You won't have to worry about her anymore."

Maia had told Jo about everything that had gone on between Chloe and herself. Her editor wasn't impressed to learn the tactics that the other writer had used to undermine Maia. "Thanks, Jo. There was something I wanted to talk to you about too. I'll give you a call in a few days."

"Make it a week or two. You two deserve a proper honeymoon. Not somewhere you're trapped together."

If she only knew how those storms had helped them.

Jo gave them both a hug and wobbled back to her table where a handsome man welcomed her back with a grin.

Maia would have to ask about that later.

Tomas kissed Maia on the cheek and clapped Alex on the shoulder. "I wish you both every happiness."

"Thank you, my friend." Alex smiled warmly.

Maia knew that Tomas would find someone who would be perfect for him. She just wasn't the one.

A quick hug and a promise to see each other soon, then Tomas hurried through the room to sit at the table next to a raven-haired beauty. Obviously, he was already on the search for his Ms. Right. It made her smile even more.

* * * *

After an amazing meal, Alex pulled his new bride out of her seat and led the way to the dance floor. With a spin, he enveloped her in his arms. "So was it everything you hoped it would be?"

Judging from her dreamy smile, he knew he'd done well. "Everything and more. It was" — she waved at the room around them — "it *is* incredible."

"Good." He would do everything in his power to give her whatever she wanted. Always. Her dream wedding was just the tip of the iceberg. He spun her again and brought her back close. The dress she had chosen was simple, elegant. The silk clung to curves that he noticed were just beginning to change. Ones that he wanted to be exploring right now.

"Hey. I know that look. We're not about to disappear into a storage closet somewhere." She kissed away his pout. If she was trying to take his mind off dragging her away? And tearing that dress off her, licking his bottom lip as she pulled back was not the way to do it.

He growled against her lips. "If you don't stop that, I'm going to embarrass us both."

Her tinkling laughter made him smile more. Watching her throughout the day, he could see that she was brimming with happiness. It was all he wanted for her. That he had been the one to provide all that made her glow the way she did made his chest swell with pride.

His gaze trailed down, past her happy smile, down the graceful curve of her neck, to the swell of her breasts...

Then Maia said something he didn't catch.

"Sorry?"

She looked up at her new husband, devastatingly handsome in his tux. As the night continued it was getting harder and harder not to drag him to the suite waiting for them upstairs. But they had to put in some time, it was their wedding after all. Though the way he looked at her put a severe dent in her best intentions.

Especially when he pulled her in close and she could feel just how eager he was to go upstairs as well.

Everything about the day had been perfect. And she knew that he would do his best to make all the days that followed the same.

They just had to endure it a little longer.

She just had to keep her mind away from dangerous thoughts, like how easy it would be to nibble his chin and slide her hands into his shirt. Or drag her hands through his hair to give it that mussed bedhead look she loved seeing on him. Or kiss those delicious lips…

She had to stop or she would be the one dragging him out. Maia looked around the room for something to distract herself. She caught Guillaume's indulgent smile and it reminded her of earlier.

"Are you going to tell me what your father said?"

He started guiltily. "Sorry?"

Amused that she'd caught Alex staring at her cleavage, she laughed. "Your father. When he came to our table. He said something to you."

Laughing, Alex lowered her into a dip. "He said he can't wait until we tell him the reason why we were toasting with ginger ale instead of champagne."

She should have known Guillaume would have noticed. The man was as astute as his son. When he swung her back up, she met his grin with her own.

"We'll tell him soon."

Alex nodded. "Maybe next week? At the opening of the new hotel in Bangkok, perhaps? We could tell him after the celebratory banquet."

Maia rolled her eyes. "You do realize it's monsoon season, right?"

He chuckled and wrapped his arms around her. "I'm sure we'll find a way to occupy the rainy days."

Knowing their luck when it came to weather, they'd have to. Laughing, she kissed him as deeply as she dared in front of witnesses. "I have no doubt."

About the Author

Kait was born and raised in the wilderness of the Pacific Northwest and started writing to entertain herself during the long winters as a child. Insatiably curious with a love of learning new things, she's picked up many random skills including three languages and two martial arts. After travelling three continents (the other four are on her bucket list), she settled in England with her family where she spends most of her time cultivating her daughter's love of reading and writing, scribbling ideas on every available scrap of paper, and trying out dialogue on her cat.

Kait loves to hear from readers. You can find her contact information, website details and author profile page at http://www.totallybound.com.

TOTALLY
BOUND

Home of Erotic Romance